Michael Ondaatje

VINTAGE **ONDAATJE**

Michael Ondaatje is the author of four novels—
Coming Through Slaughter, the story of the New Orleans
jazz musician Buddy Bolden, *In the Skin of a Lion*,
which is set in Toronto, *The English Patient*, and *Anil's
Ghost*. His memoir, *Running in the Family*, is about his
family in Sri Lanka, where he was born. He has also
written several books of poetry, including *The Collected Works of Billy the Kid*, *There's a Trick with a Knife
I'm Learning to Do*, *Secular Love*, *The Cinnamon Peeler*,
and *Handwriting*. His novel *The English Patient* won
the Booker Prize and *Anil's Ghost* won the Irish Times
International Fiction Award, the Giller Award, and
the Prix Medicis. Both works won the Governor
General Award. His most recent work is *The Conversations: Walter Murch and the Art of Editing Film*. He has
been an editor for Coach House Press and the Canadian literary magazine *BRICK*. He lives in Toronto,
Canada.

Prose

Coming Through Slaughter (1976)
Running in the Family (memoir) (1982)
In the Skin of a Lion (1987)
The English Patient (1992)
Anil's Ghost (2000)

Poetry

The Dainty Monsters (1967)
The Man with Seven Toes (1969)
The Collected Works of Billy the Kid (1970)
Rat Jelly (1973)
Elimination Dance (1976)
Claude Glass (1979)
There's a Trick with a Knife I'm Learning to Do (1979)
Tin Roof (1982)
Secular Love (1984)
The Cinnamon Peeler (1991)
Handwriting (1998)

Nonfiction

*The Conversations: Walter Murch and the Art
of Editing Film*

VINTAGE ONDAATJE

Michael Ondaatje

VINTAGE BOOKS

A Division of Random House, Inc.

New York

Selection from The Collected Works of Billy the Kid, *copyright © 1970 by Michael
Ondaatje.* "Light," "Claude Glass," "The Cinnamon Peeler," "Elimination Dance," *and* "To a
Sad Daughter" *from* The Cinnamon Peeler, *copyright © 1989, 1991 by Michael Ondaatje.
Selection from* Coming Through Slaughter, *copyright © 1976 by Michael Ondaatje.* "Travels in Ceylon," "The Passions of Lalla," *and* "Photograph" *from* Running in the Family,
copyright © 1982 by Michael Ondaatje. "The Bridge" *from* In the Skin of a Lion, *copyright
© 1987 by Michael Ondaatje.* "Katharine" *and* "In Situ" *from* The English Patient, *copyright © 1992 by Michael Ondaatje.* "The Great Tree," "The Story," "Step," *and* "Last Ink"
from Handwriting, *copyright © 1998 by Michael Ondaatje.* "Linus Corea" *and* "Anil" *from*
Anil's Ghost, *copyright © 2000 by Michael Ondaatje.*

Library of Congress Cataloging-in-Publication Data
Ondaatje, Michael, 1943–
Vintage Ondaatje / Michael Ondaatje.
p. cm.
"A Vintage original"—T.p. verso.
ISBN 1-4000-7744-3
I. Title.
PR9199.3.O5 A6 2004
818'.54—dc22
2004052609

Book design by JoAnne Metsch

www.vintagebooks.com

Printed in the United States of America
10 9 8 7 6 5 4 3 2 1

CONTENTS

VINTAGE **ONDAATJE**

These are the killed.

(By me)—
Morton, Baker, early friends of mine.
Joe Bernstein. 3 Indians.
A blacksmith when I was twelve, with a knife.
5 Indians in self defence (behind a very safe rock).
One man who bit me during a robbery.
Brady, Hindman, Beckwith, Joe Clark,
Deputy Jim Carlyle, Deputy Sheriff J. W. Bell.
And Bob Ollinger. A rabid cat
birds during practice,

These are the killed.

(By them)—
Charlie, Tom O'Folliard
Angela D's split arm,
                    and Pat Garrett
sliced off my head.
Blood a necklace on me all my life.

Christmas at Fort Sumner, 1880. There were five of us together then. Wilson, Dave Rudabaugh, Charlie Bowdre, Tom O'Folliard, and me. In November we celebrated my 21st birthday, mixing red dirt and alcohol—a public breathing throughout the night. The next day we were told that Pat Garrett had been made sheriff and had accepted it. We were bad for progress in New Mexico and cattle politicians like Chisum wanted the bad name out. They made Garrett sheriff and he sent me a letter saying move out or I will get you Billy. The government sent a Mr. Azariah F. Wild to help him out. Between November and December I killed Jim Carlyle over some mixup, he being a friend.

Tom O'Folliard decided to go east then, said he would meet up with us in Sumner for Christmas. Goodbye goodbye. A few days before Christmas we were told that Garrett was in Sumner waiting for us all. Christmas night. Garrett, Mason, Wild, with four or five others. Tom O'Folliard rides into town, leaning his rifle between the horse's ears. He would shoot from the waist now which, with a rifle, was pretty good, and he was always accurate.

Garrett had been waiting for us, playing poker with the others, guns on the floor beside them. Told that Tom was riding in alone, he went straight to the window and shot O'Folliard's horse dead. Tom collapsed with the horse still holding the gun and blew out Garrett's window. Garrett already halfway downstairs. Mr. Wild shot at Tom from the other side of the street, rather unnecessarily shooting the horse again. If Tom had used stirrups and didn't swing his legs so much he would probably have been locked under the animal. O'Folliard moved soon. When Garrett had got to ground level, only the horse was there in the open street, good and dead. He couldn't shout to ask Wild where O'Folliard was or he would've got busted. Wild started to yell to tell Garrett though and Tom killed him at once. Garrett fired at O'Folliard's flash and took his shoulder off. Tom O'Folliard screaming out onto the quiet Fort Sumner street, Christmas night, walking over to Garrett, no shoulder left, his jaws tilting up and down like mad bladders going. Too mad to even aim at Garrett. Son of a bitch son of a bitch, as Garrett took clear aim and blew him out.

Garrett picked him up, the head broken in two, took him back upstairs into the hotel room. Mason stretched out a blanket neat in the corner. Garrett placed Tom O'Folliard down, broke open Tom's rifle, took the remaining shells and placed them by him. They had to wait till morning now. They continued their poker game till six a.m. Then remembered they hadn't done anything about Wild. So the four of them went out, brought Wild into the room. At eight in the morning Garrett buried Tom O'Folliard. He had known him quite well. Then he went to the train station, put Azariah F. Wild on ice and sent him back to Washington.

The barn I stayed in for a week then was at the edge of a farm and had been deserted it seemed for several years, though built of stone and good wood. The cold dark grey of the place made my eyes become used to soft light and I burned out my fever there. It was twenty yards long, about ten yards wide. Above me was another similar sized room but the floors were unsafe for me to walk on. However I heard birds and the odd animal scrape their feet, the rotten wood magnifying the sound so they entered my dreams and nightmares.

But it was the colour and light of the place that made me stay there, not my fever. It became a calm week. It was the colour and the light. The colour a grey with remnants of brown—for instance those rust brown pipes and metal objects that before had held bridles or pails, that slid to machine uses; the thirty or so grey cans in one corner of the room, their ellipses, from where I sat, setting up patterns in the dark.

When I had arrived I opened two windows and a door and the sun poured blocks and angles in, lighting up the floor's skin of feathers and dust and old grain. The windows looked out onto fields and plants grew at the door, me killing them gradually with my urine. Wind came in wet and brought in birds who flew to the other end of the room to get their aim to fly out again. An old tap hung from the roof, the same colour as the walls, so once I knocked myself out on it.

For that week then I made a bed of the table there and lay out my fever, whatever it was. I began to block my mind of all thought. Just sensed the room and learnt what my body could do, what it could survive, what colours it liked best, what songs I sang best. There were animals who did not move out and accepted me as a larger breed. I ate the old grain with them, drank from a constant puddle about twenty yards away from the barn. I saw no human and heard no human voice, learned to squat the best way when shitting, used leaves for wiping, never ate flesh or touched another animal's flesh, never entered his boundary. We were all aware and allowed each other. The fly who sat on my arm, after his inquiry, just went away, ate his disease and kept it in him. When I walked I avoided the cobwebs who had places to grow to, who had stories to finish. The flies caught in those acrobat nets were the only murder I saw.

And in the barn next to us there was another granary, separated by just a thick wood door. In it a hundred or so rats, thick rats, eating and eating the foot deep pile of grain abandoned now and fermenting so that at the end of my week, after a heavy rain storm burst the power in those seeds and brought drunkenness into the minds of those rats, they abandoned the sanity of eating the food before them and turned on each other and grotesque and awkwardly because of their size they went for each other's eyes and ribs so the yellow stomachs slid out and they came through that door and killed a chipmunk—about ten of them onto that one striped thing and the ten eating each other before they realised the chipmunk was long gone so that I, sitting on the open window with its thick sill where they couldn't reach me, filled my gun and fired again and again into their slow wheel across the room at each boommm, and reloaded and fired again and again till I went through the whole bag of bullet supplies—the noise breaking out the seal of silence in my ears, the smoke sucked out of the window as it emerged from my fist and the long twenty yard space between me and them empty but for the floating bullet lonely as an emissary across and between the wooden posts that never returned, so the rats continued to wheel and stop in the silences and eat each other, some even the bullet. Till my hand was black and the gun was hot and no other animal of any kind remained in that room but for the boy in the blue shirt sitting there coughing at the dust, rubbing the sweat of his upper lip with his left forearm.

After shooting Gregory
this is what happened

I'd shot him well and careful
made it explode under his heart
so it wouldn't last long and
was about to walk away
when this chicken paddles out to him
and as he was falling hops on his neck
digs the beak into his throat
straightens legs and heaves
a red and blue vein out

Meanwhile he fell
and the chicken walked away

still tugging at the vein
till it was 12 yards long
as if it held that body like a kite
Gregory's last words being

get away from me yer stupid chicken

January at Tivan Arroyo, called Stinking Springs more often. With me, Charlie, Wilson, Dave Rudabaugh. Snow. Charlie took my hat and went out to get wood and feed the horses. The shot burnt the clothes on his stomach off and lifted him right back into the room. Snow on Charlie's left boot. He had taken one step out. In one hand had been an axe, in the other a pail. No guns.

Get up Charlie, get up, go and get one. No Billy. I'm tired, please. Jesus watch your hands Billy. Get up Charlie. I prop him to the door, put his gun in his hand. Take off, good luck Charlie.

He stood there weaving, not moving. Then began to walk in a perfect, incredible straight line out of the door towards Pat and the others at the ridge of the arroyo about twenty yards away. He couldn't even lift his gun. Moving sideways at times but always always in a straight line. Dead on Garrett. Shoot him Charlie. They were watching him only, not moving. Over his shoulder I aimed at Pat, fired, and hit his shoulder braid. Hadn't touched him. Charlie hunched. Get up Charlie kill him kill him. Charlie got up poking the gun barrel in snow. Went straight towards Garrett. The others had ducked down, but not Garrett who just stood there and I didn't shoot again. Charlie he knew was already dead now, had to go somewhere, do something, to get his mind off the pain. Charlie went straight, now closer to them his hands covered the mess in his trousers. Shoot him Charlie shoot him. The blood trail he left straight as a knife cut.

Getting there getting there. Charlie getting to the arroyo, pitching into Garrett's arms, slobbering his stomach on Garrett's gun belt. Hello Charlie, said Pat quietly.

Snow outside. Wilson, Dave Rudabaugh and me. No windows, the door open so we could see. Four horses outside.

Pat Garrett, ideal assassin. Public figure, the mind of a doctor, his hands hairy, scarred, burned by rope, on his wrist there was a purple stain there all his life. Ideal assassin for his mind was unwarped. Had the ability to kill someone on the street walk back and finish a joke. One who had decided what was right and forgot all morals. He was genial to everyone even his enemies. He genuinely enjoyed people, some who were odd, the dopes, the thieves. Most dangerous for them, he understood them, what motivated their laughter and anger, what they liked to think about, how he had to act for them to like him. An academic murderer—only his vivacious humour and diverse interests made him the best kind of company. He would listen to people like Rudabaugh and giggle at their escapades. His language was atrocious in public, yet when alone he never swore.

At the age of 15 he taught himself French and never told anyone about it and never spoke to anyone in French for the next 40 years. He didn't even read French books.

Between the ages of 15 and 18 little was heard of Garrett. In Juan Para he bought himself a hotel room for two years with money he had saved and organised a schedule to learn how to drink. In the first three months he forced himself to disintegrate his mind. He would vomit everywhere. In a year he could drink two bottles a day and not vomit. He began to dream for the first time in his life. He would wake up in the mornings, his sheets soaked in urine 40% alcohol. He became frightened of flowers because they grew so slowly that he couldn't tell what they planned to do. His mind learned to be superior because of the excessive mistakes of those around him. Flowers watched him.

After two years he could drink anything, mix anything together and stay awake and react just as effectively as when sober. But he was now addicted, locked in his own game. His money was running out. He had planned the drunk to last only two years, now it continued into new months over which he had no control. He stole and sold himself to survive. One day he was robbing the house of Juanita Martinez, was discovered by her, and collapsed in her living room. In about six months she had un-iced his addiction. They married and two weeks later she died of a consumption she had hidden from him.

What happened in Garrett's mind no one knows. He did not drink, was never seen. A month after Juanita Garrett's death he arrived in Sumner.

PAULITA MAXWELL: *I remember the first day Pat Garrett ever set foot in Fort Sumner. I was a small girl with dresses at my shoe-tops and when he came to our house and asked for a job, I stood behind my brother Pete and stared at him in open eyed wonder; he had the longest legs I'd ever seen and he looked so comical and had such a droll way of talking that after he was gone, Pete and I had a good laugh about him.*

His mind was clear, his body able to drink, his feelings, unlike those who usually work their own way out of hell, not cynical about another's incapacity to get out of problems and difficulties. He did ten years of ranching, cow punching, being a buffalo hunter. He married Apolinaria Guitterrez and had five sons. He had come to Sumner then, mind full of French he never used, everything equipped to be that rare thing—a sane assassin sane assassin sane assassin sane assassin sane assassin sane

Got here this afternoon. Walk around remembering you from the objects I find. Books, pictures on the wall, nail holes in the ceiling where you've hung your magnets, seed packets on the shelf above the sink—the skin you shed when you finish your vacations. Re-smell your character.

Not enough blankets here, Webb, and it's cold. Found an old hunting jacket. I sleep against its cloth full of hunter sweat, aroma of cartridges. I went to bed as soon as I arrived and am awake now after midnight. Scratch of suicide at the side of my brain.

Our friendship had nothing accidental did it. Even at the start you set out to breed me into something better. Which you did. You removed my immaturity at just the right time and saved me a lot of energy and I sped away happy and alone in a new town away from you, and now you produce a leash, curl the leather round and round your fist, and walk straight into me. And you pull me home. Like those breeders of bull terriers in the Storyville pits who can

prove anything of their creatures, can prove how determined their dogs are by setting them onto an animal and
while the jaws clamp shut they can slice the dog's body in
half knowing the jaws will not let go.

All the time I hate what I am doing and want the other.
In a room full of people I get frantic in their air and their
shout and when I'm alone I sniff the smell of their bodies
against my clothes. I'm scared Webb, don't think I will find
one person who will be the right audience. All you've
done is cut me in half, pointing me here. Where I don't
want these answers.

*

I go outside and piss in your garden. When I get back onto
the porch the dog is licking at the waterbowl trying to
avoid the yellow leaves floating in it. With all the time in
the world he moves his body into perfect manoeuvering
position so he can get his tongue between the yellow and
reach the invisible water. His tongue curls and captures it.
He enters the house with me, the last mouthful pouring
out of his jaws. Once inside he rushes around so the cold
night air caught in his hair falls off his body.

The dog follows me wherever I go now. If I am slow
walking he runs ahead and waits looking back. If I piss
outside he comes to the area, investigates, and pisses in the
same place, then scratches earth over it. Once he even came
over to the wet spot and covered it up without doing anything himself. Today I watched him carefully and returned

the compliment. After he had leaked against a tree I went over, pissed there too, and scuffed my shoe against the earth so he would know I had his system. He was delighted. He barked loud and ran round me excited for a few minutes. He must have felt there had been a major breakthrough in the spread of hound civilization and who knows he may be right. How about that Webb, a little sensa humour to show you.

★

Tired. Sulphur. When you're tired, the body thick, you smell sulphur. Bellocq did that. Always. Two in the morning three in the morning against the window of the street restaurant he'd rub a match on the counter and sniff it in. Ammonia ripping into his brain. Jarring out the tiredness. And then back to his conversations about everything except music, the friend who scorned all the giraffes of fame. I said, You don't think much of this music do you? Not yet, he said. Him watching me waste myself and wanting me to step back into my body as if into a black room and stumble against whatever was there. Unable then to be watched by others. More and more I said he was wrong and more and more I spent whole evenings with him.

The small tired man sitting on the restaurant bench or the barber chair never saying his scorn but just his boredom at what I was trying to do. And me in my vanity accusing him at first of being tone deaf! He was offering me black empty spaces. Revived himself with matches once an hour, wanted me to become blind to everything but the owned pain in myself. And so yes there is a need to come home Webb with that casual desert blackness.

Whatever I say about him you will interpret as the working of an enemy and what I loved Webb were the possibilities in his silence. He was just *there*, like a small noon shadow. Dear Bellocq, he was so short he was the only one who could stretch up in the barber shop and not get hit by the fan. He didn't rely on anything. He trusted nothing, not even me. I can't summarize him for you, he tempted me out of the world of audiences where I had tried to catch everything thrown at me. He offered mole comfort, mole deceit. Come with me Webb I want to show you something, no come with me I want to *show* you something. You come too. Put your hand through this window.

*

You didn't know me for instance when I was with the Brewitts, without Nora. Three of us played cards all evening and then Jaelin would stay downstairs and Robin and I would go to bed, me with his wife. He would be alone and silent downstairs. Then eventually he would sit down and press into the teeth of the piano. His practice reached us upstairs, each note a finger on our flesh. The unheard tap of his calloused fingers and the muscle reaching into the machine and plucking the note, the sound travelling up the stairs and through the door, touching her on the shoulder. The music was his dance in the auditorium of enemies. But I loved him downstairs as much as she loved the man downstairs. God, to sit down and play, to tip it over into music! To remove the anger and stuff it down the piano fresh every night. He would wait for half an hour as dogs wait for masters to go to sleep before they move into the garbage of the kitchen. The music was so uncertain it was heartbreaking and beautiful. Coming through the walls. The lost anger at her or me or himself. Bullets of music delivered onto the bed we were on.

Everybody's love in the air.

*

For two hours I've been listening to a radio I discovered in your cupboard of clothes. Under old pyjamas. You throw nothing away. Nightshirts, belts, some coins, and sitting in the midst of them all the radio. The wiring old. I had to push it into a socket, nervous, ready to jump back. But the metal slid in and connected and the buzz that gradually warmed up came from a long distance away into this room.

For two hours I've been listening. People talking about a crisis I missed that has been questionably solved. Couldn't understand it. They were not being clear, they were not giving me the history of it all, and I didn't know who was supposed to be the hero of the story. So I've been hunched up on the bed listening to voices, and then later on Robichaux's band came on.

John Robichaux! Playing his waltzes. And I hate to admit it but I enjoyed listening to the clear forms. Every note part of the large curve, so carefully patterned that for the first time I appreciated the possibilities of a mind moving ahead of the instruments in time and waiting with pleasure for them to catch up. I had never been aware of that mechanistic pleasure, that trust.

Did you ever meet Robichaux? I never did. I loathed everything he stood for. He dominated his audiences. He put his emotions into patterns which a listening crowd had to follow. My enjoyment tonight was because I wanted something that was just a utensil. Had a bath, washed my hair, and wanted the same sort of clarity and open-headedness. But I don't believe it for a second. You may perhaps but it is not real. When I played parades we would be going down Canal Street and at each intersection people would hear just the fragment I happened to be playing and it would fade as I went further down Canal. They would not be there to hear the end of phrases, Robichaux's arches. I wanted them to be able to come in where they pleased and leave when they pleased and somehow hear the germs of the start and all the possible endings at whatever point in the music that I had reached *then*. Like your radio without the beginnings or endings. The right ending is an open door you can't see too far out of. It can mean exactly the opposite of what you are thinking.

An abrupt station shut down. Voices said goodnight several times and the orchestra playing in the background collapsed into buzz again, a few yards away from me in your bedroom.

*

My fathers were those who put their bodies over barbed wire. For me. To slide over into the region of hell. Through their sacrifice they seduced me into the game. They showed me their autographed pictures and they told me about their women and they told me of the even bigger names all over the country. My fathers failing. Dead before they hit the wire.

There were three of them. Mutt Carey, Bud Scott, Happy Galloway. Don't know what they taught me for the real teachers never teach you craft. In a way the stringmen taught me more than Carey and his trumpet. Or Manuel Hall who lived with my mother in his last years and hid his trumpet in the cupboard and never touched it when anyone was around. It was good when you listened to Galloway bubble underneath the others and come through slipping and squealing into neighbourhoods that had nothing to do with the thumper tunes coming out of the rest. His guitar much closer to the voice than the other instruments. It swallowed moods and kept three or four going at the same time which was what I wanted. While the trumpet was usually the steel shoe you couldn't get out of because you led the music and there was an end you had to get to. But Galloway's guitar was everything else that needn't have been there but was put there by him, worshipful, brushing against strange weeds. So Galloway taught me not craft but to play a mood of sound I would recognize and remember. Every note new and raw and chance. Never repeated. His mouth also moving and trying to mime the sound but never able to for his brain had lost control of his fingers.

In mirror to him Carey's trumpet was a technician—which went gliding down river and missed all the shit on the bottom. His single strong notes pelting out into the crowds, able to reach any note that he wished for but always reaching for the purest. He was orange juice he was exercise, you understand. He was a wheel on a king's coach. So that was technique.

Drawn to opposites, even in music we play. In terror we lean in the direction that is most unlike us. Running past your own character into pain. So they died eventually maybe suiciding for me or failing because of a lost lip who knows. Climbing over them still with me in the sense I have tried all my life to avoid becoming them. Galloway in his lovely suits playing his bubble music under shit bands— so precise off the platform so completely alone in his music he wished to persuade no one into his style, and forgotten by everyone who saw him. A dull person off stage. And he'd lie and make himself even duller to keep people away from him. Who remembers him? Even I forgot him for so long until now. Till you ask these questions. He slipped back into my memory as accidentally as a smell. All my ancestors died drunk or lost but Galloway continued to play till he died and when he failed to show up was replaced. Had a stroke during breakfast at sixty-five and was forgotten. So immaculate when he fell against his chair even the undertaker could not improve on him.

So I suppose I crawled over him.

And Scott who kept losing his career to neurotic women.

And Carey who lost his hard lip too young and slept himself to death with the money he made. Floating around the bars to hear good music, having a good time and then died. Attracted to opposites again, to the crazy music he chose to die listening to, bitching at new experiments, the chaos, but refusing to leave the table and go down the street and listen to captive jazz he himself had generated. A dog turned wild in pasture.

He was my father too in the way he visited me and Nora at the end. Not liking my music damning my music but moving in for a month or so before he died, trying to make passes at my pregnant wife by getting up early in the morning when she got up and I was still in bed or in a bath. Perhaps even hurt by me not bothering to be jealous because I took my time getting downstairs. We would fight about everything. Even the way I held the cornet or shouted out in the middle of numbers. And still he'd come every night and listen and be irritated and enjoy himself tremendously. And then one morning in the room he shared with my first kid he stayed in bed and shook and shook, unable to move anything except for those massive shoulders. Arms struck dead. Get the sweat out of my eyes get the sweat out of my eyes fuckit I'm going to die, and then dead in the middle of a shake. I leaned over his wet body and put an ear to his mouth wanting more than anything then to hear his air, the swirl of air in him but there was none. His open mouth was an old sea-shell. I turned my head slowly and kissed the soft old lips. I then went over the barbed wire attached to his heart.

The black dog I picked up a few miles south of your place
has snuggled against me. No woman for over a month has
been as close to my body as he is tonight. I got up to make
a drink and returned to find him sitting on the sofa where
my warmth had been. Dogs on your furniture, Webb. He
is quite dirty and I'll bathe him tomorrow. Just dusty for
the most part but there are pointed knots of mud under the
belly—probably collected by going through wet evening
grass. He is not used to living in houses I can tell, although
he immediately climbs onto furniture. He is not used to
softness and every few hours throughout the night he
moves from chair to sofa and finally finds the floor to be
the answer. I came back into the room and he looked up
expecting me to reclaim my place. I've snuggled against his
warmth. Have just bent over and notice his claws are torn.

The heat has fallen back into the lake and left air empty.
You can smell trees across the bay. I notice tonight someone has moved in over there. One square of light came on
at twilight and changed the gentle shape of the tree line,
making the horizon invisible. Was annoyed till I admitted
to myself I had been lonely and this comforted me. The
rest of the world is in that cabin room behind the light.
Everyone I know lives there and when the light is on it
means they are there. Before, every animal noise made me
suspect people were arriving. Rain would sound like tires
on the gravel. I would run out my heart furious and thump-
ing only to be surrounded by a sudden downpour. I would
stand shaking, getting completely wet for over a minute.

Then come in, strip all my clothes off and crouch in front of the fire.

Webb I'm tired of the bitching tonight. The loneliness. I really wanted to talk about my friends. Nora and Pickett and me. Robin and Jaelin and me. I saw an awful thing among us. And that was passion could twist around and choose someone else just like that. That in one minute I knew Nora loved me and then, whatever I did from a certain day on, her eyes were hunting Pickett's mouth and silence. There was nothing I could do. Pickett could just stand there and he had her heart balanced on his tongue. And then with Robin and me—Jaelin stood there far more intelligent and sensitive and loving and pained and it did nothing to her, she had swerved to me like a mad compass, aimed east east east, ignoring everything else. I knew I was hurting him and I screwed her and at times humiliated her in front of him, everything. We had no order among ourselves. I wouldn't let myself control the world of my music because I had no power over anything else that went on around me, in or around my body. My wife loved Pickett, I think. I loved Robin Brewitt, I think. We were all exhausted.

*

From the very first night I was lost from Robin.

The cold in my head and the cough woke me. Walking round your house making hot water grapefruit and Raleigh Rye drinks. That was the first night that was four weeks ago. And now too my starving avoiding food. Drunk and hungry in the middle of the night in this place crowded with your furniture and my muttering voice. Robin lost. Who slid out of my heart. Who has become anonymous as cloud. I wake up with erections in memory of Robin. Every morning. Till she has begun to blur into Nora and everybody else.

What do you want to know about me Webb? I'm alone. I desire every woman I remember. Everything is clear here and still I feel my brain has walked away and is watching me. I feel I hover over the objects in this house, over every person in my memory—like those painted saints in my mother's church who seem to always have six or seven inches between them and the ground. Posing as humans. I give myself immaculate twenty minute shaves in the morning. Tap some lotion on me and cook a fabulous breakfast. Only meal of the day. So I move from the morning's energy into the later hours of alcohol and hunger and thickness and tiredness. Trying to overcome this awful and stupid clarity.

After breakfast I train. Mouth and lips and breathing. Exercises. Scales. For hours till my jaws and stomach ache. But no music or tune that I long to play. Just the notes, can you understand that? It is like perfecting 100 yard starts and stopping after the third yard and back again to the beginning. In this way the notes jerk forward in a spurt.

Alone now three weeks, four weeks? Since you came to Shell Beach and found me. Come back you said. All that music. I don't want that way any more. There is this other path I beat the bushes away from with exercise so I can walk down it knowing it is just stone. I've got more theoretical with no one to talk to. All suicides all acts of privacy are romantic you say and you may be right, as I sit here at 4.45 in the middle of the night, sky beginning to emerge blue through darkness into the long big windows of this house. Here's an early morning ant crossing the table . . .

Three days ago Crawley visited me. I made you promise not to say where I was but you sent him here anyway. He came in his car, interrupted my thinking and it has taken me a couple of days to get back. With a girl fan he came in his car and played some music he's working on, while she was silent and touching in the corner. I could have done without his music, I could have done with her body. Music quite good but I could have finished it for him, it was a memory. I wanted to start a fight. I was watching her while he was playing and I wanted the horn in her skirt. I wanted her to sit with her skirt on my cock like a bandage. My old friend's girl. What have you brought me back to Webb?

The day got better with the opening of bottles and all of us were vaguely drunk by the time they left and me rambling on as they were about to leave, leaning against the driver's window apologizing, explaining what I wanted to do. About the empty room when I get up and put metal onto my mouth and hit the squawk at just the right note to equal the tone of the room and that's all you do. Pushing all that into the car as if we had a minute to live as if we hadn't talked rubbish all day.

You learn to play like that and no band will play with you, he says.

I know. I want to get this conversation right and I'm drunk and I'm making it difficult.

Shouting into his car, standing on the pebble driveway, the sweat on me which is really alcohol gone through me and bubbled out. I said I didn't want to be a remnant, a ladder for others. So Crawley knowing, nodding. I ask him about Nora, tells me that she's living with Cornish. And I've always thought of her as sad Nora, and my children, all this soft private sentiment I forgot to explode, the kids who grow up without me quite capable, while I sit out this drunk sweat, thinking along a stone path. I am terrified now of their lost love. I walk around the car put my head in to kiss Crawley's girl whose name I cannot even remember, my tongue in her cool mouth, her cool circling answer that gives me an erection against the car door, and round the car again and look at Crawley and thank him for the bottles he brought. His brain with me for two days afterwards.

Alcohol sweat on these pages. I am tired Webb. I put my forehead down to rest on the booklet on the table. I don't want to get up. When I lift my head up the paper will be damp, the ink spread. The lake and sky will be light blue. Not even her cloud.

Ceylon falls on a map and its outline is the shape of a tear. After the spaces of India and Canada it is so small. A miniature. Drive ten miles and you are in a landscape so different that by rights it should belong to another country. From Galle in the south to Colombo a third of the way up the coast is only seventy miles. When houses were built along the coastal road it was said that a chicken could walk between the two cities without touching ground. The country is cross-hatched with maze-like routes whose only escape is the sea. From a ship or plane you can turn back or look down at the disorder. Villages spill onto streets, the jungle encroaches on village.

The Ceylon Road and Rail Map resembles a small garden full of darting red and black birds. In the middle of the 19th century, a 17-year-old English officer was ordered to organize the building of a road from Colombo to Kandy. Workers tore paths out of the sides of mountains and hacked through jungle, even drilled a huge hole through a rock on the hairpin bend of the Kadugannawa Pass. It was finished when the officer was thirty-six. There was a lot of this sort of casual obsession going on at that time.

My father, too, seemed fated to have an obsession with trains all his life. Rail trips became his nemesis. If one was to be blind drunk in the twenties and thirties, one somehow managed it on public transport, or on roads that would terrify a sober man with mountain passes, rock cuts, and precipices. Being an officer in the Ceylon Light Infantry, my father was allowed free train passes and became notorious on the Colombo-Trincomalee run.

He began quietly enough. In his twenties he pulled out his army pistol, terrified a fellow officer—John Kotelawala— under his seat, walked through the swaying carriages and threatened to kill the driver unless he stopped the train. The train halted ten miles out of Colombo at seven-thirty in the morning. He explained that he expected this trip to be a pleasant one and he wanted his good friend Arthur van Langenberg who had missed the train to enjoy it with him.

The passengers emptied out to wait on the tracks while a runner was sent back to Colombo to get Arthur. After a two-hour delay Arthur arrived, John Kotelawala came out from under his seat, everyone jumped back on, my father put his pistol away, and the train continued on to Trincomalee.

I think my father believed that he owned the railway by birthright. He wore the railway as if it was a public suit of clothes. Trains in Ceylon lack privacy entirely. There are no individual compartments, and most of the passengers spend their time walking through carriages, curious to see who else is on board. So people usually knew when Mervyn

Ondaatje boarded the train, with or without his army revolver. (He tended to stop trains more often when in uniform.) If the trip coincided with his days of dipsomania the train could be delayed for hours. Messages would be telegraphed from one station to another to arrange for a relative to meet and remove him from the train. My uncle Noel was usually called. As he was in the Navy during the war, a naval jeep would roar towards Anuradhapura to pick up the major from the Ceylon Light Infantry.

When my father removed all his clothes and leapt from the train, rushing into the Kadugannawa tunnel, the Navy finally refused to follow and my mother was sent for. He stayed in the darkness of that three-quarter-mile-long tunnel for three hours stopping rail traffic going both ways. My mother, clutching a suit of civilian clothing (the Army would not allow her to advertise his military connections), walked into that darkness, finding him and talking with him for over an hour and a half. A moment only Conrad could have interpreted. She went in there alone, his clothes in one arm—but no shoes, an oversight he later complained of—and a railway lantern that he shattered as soon as she reached him. They had been married for six years.

They survived that darkness. And my mother, the lover of Tennyson and early Yeats, began to realize that she had caught onto a different breed of dog. She was to become tough and valiant in a very different world from then on, determined, when they divorced, never to ask him for money, and to raise us all on her own earnings. They were both from gracious, genteel families, but my father went down a path unknown to his parents and wife. She followed him and coped with him for fourteen years, surrounding his behaviour like a tough and demure breeze. Talking him out of suicide in a three-quarter-mile-long tunnel, for god's sake! She walked in armed with clothes she had borrowed from another passenger, and a light, and her knowledgeable love of all the beautiful formal poetry that existed up to the 1930s, to meet her naked husband in the darkness, in the black slow breeze of the Kadugannawa tunnel, unable to find him until he rushed at her, grabbed that lantern and dashed it against the wall before he realized who it was, who had come for him.

"It's me!"

Then a pause. And, "How *dare* you follow me!"

"I followed you because no one else would follow you."

If you look at my mother's handwriting from the thirties on, it has changed a good deal from her youth. It looks wild, drunk, the letters are much larger and billow over the pages, almost as if she had changed hands. Reading her letters we thought that the blue aerograms were written in ten seconds flat. But once my sister saw her writing and it was the most laboured process, her tongue twisting in her mouth. As if that scrawl was the result of great discipline, as if at the age of thirty or so she had been blasted, forgotten how to write, lost the use of a habitual style and forced herself to cope with a new dark unknown alphabet.

*

Resthouses are an old tradition in Ceylon. The roads are so dangerous that there is one every fifteen miles. You can drive in to relax, have a drink or lunch or get a room for the night. Between Colombo and Kandy people stop at the Kegalle resthouse; from Colombo to Hatton, they stop at the Kitulgala resthouse. This was my father's favourite.

It was on his travels by road that my father waged war with a certain Sammy Dias Bandaranaike, a close relative of the eventual Prime Minister of Ceylon who was assassinated by a Buddhist monk.

It is important to understand the tradition of the Visitors' Book. After a brief or long stay at a resthouse, one is expected to write one's comments. The Bandaranaike-Ondaatje feud began and was contained within the arena of such visitors' books. What happened was that Sammy Dias Bandaranaike and my father happened to visit the Kitulgala resthouse simultaneously. Sammy Dias, or so my side of the feud tells it, was a scrounger for complaints. While most people wrote two or three curt lines, he would have spent his whole visit checking every tap and shower to see what was wrong and would have plenty to say. On this occasion, Sammy left first, having written half a page in the Kitulgala resthouse visitors' book. He bitched at everything, from the service to the badly made drinks, to the poor rice, to the bad beds. Almost an epic. My father left two hours later and wrote two sentences, "No complaints. Not even about Mr. Bandaranaike." As most people read these comments, they were as public as a newspaper advertisement, and soon everyone including Sammy had heard about it. And everyone but Sammy was amused.

A few months later they both happened to hit the rest-house in Avissawella for lunch. They stayed there only an hour ignoring each other. Sammy left first, wrote a half-page attack on my father, and complimented the good food. My father wrote one and a half pages of vindictive prose about the Bandaranaike family, dropping hints of madness and incest. The next time they came together, Sammy Dias allowed my father to write first and, after he had left, put down all the gossip he knew about the Ondaatjes.

This literary war broke so many codes that for the first time in Ceylon history pages had to be ripped out of visitors' books. Eventually one would write about the other even when the other was nowhere near the resthouse. Pages continued to be torn out, ruining a good archival history of two semi-prominent Ceylon families. The war petered out when neither Sammy Dias nor my father was allowed to write their impressions of a stay or a meal. The standard comment on visitors' books today about "constructive criticism" dates from this period.

*

My father's last train ride (he was banned from the Ceylon Railways after 1943) was his most dramatic. The year I was born he was a major with the Ceylon Light Infantry and was stationed away from my mother in Trincomalee. There were fears of a Japanese attack and he became obsessed with a possible invasion. In charge of Transport he would wake up whole battalions and rush them to various points of the harbour or coastline, absolutely certain that the Japanese would not come by plane but by ship. Marble Beach, Coral Beach, Nilaveli, Elephant Point, Frenchman's

Pass, all suddenly began to glow like fireflies from army jeeps sent there at three in the morning. He began to drink a lot, moved onto a plateau of constant alcohol, and had to be hospitalized. Authorities decided to send him back to a military hospital in Colombo under the care of John Kotelawala, once more the unfortunate travelling companion. (Sir John Kotelawala, for he was eventually to become Prime Minister.) Somehow my father smuggled bottles of gin onto the train and even before they left Trinco he was raging. The train sped through tunnels, scrubland, careened around sharp bends, and my father's fury imitated it, its speed and shake and loudness, he blew in and out of carriages, heaving bottles out of the windows as he finished them, getting John Kotelawala's gun.

More drama was taking place off the train as his relatives tried to intercept it before he reached Colombo. For some reason it was crucial that he be taken to hospital by a member of the family rather than under military guard. His sister, my Aunt Stephy, drove to meet the train at Anuradhapura, not quite sure what his condition was but sure that she was his favourite sister. Unfortunately she arrived at the station in a white silk dress, a white feathered hat, and a long white pair of gloves—perhaps to impress John Kotelawala who was in charge of her brother and who was attracted to her. Her looks gathered such a crowd and caused such an uproar that she was surrounded and couldn't reach the carriage when the train slowed into the station. John Kotelawala glanced at her with wonder—this slight, demure, beautiful woman in white on the urine-soaked platform—while he struggled with her brother who had begun to take off his clothes.

"Mervyn!"

"Stephy!"

Shouted as they passed each other, the train pulling out, Stephy still being mobbed, and an empty bottle crashing onto the end of the platform like a last sentence.

John Kotelawala was knocked out by my father before he reached Galgamuwa. He never pressed charges. In any case my father took over the train.

He made it shunt back and forth ten miles one way, ten miles another, so that all trains, some full of troops, were grounded in the south unable to go anywhere. He managed to get the driver of the train drunk as well and was finishing a bottle of gin every hour walking up and down the carriages almost naked, but keeping his shoes on this time and hitting the state of inebriation during which he would start rattling off wonderful limericks—thus keeping the passengers amused.

But there was another problem to contend with. One whole carriage was given over to high-ranking British officers. They had retired early and, while the train witnessed small revolutions among the local military, everyone felt that the anarchic events should be kept from the sleeping foreigners. The English thought Ceylon trains were bad enough, and if they discovered that officers in the Ceylon Light Infantry were going berserk and upsetting schedules they might just leave the country in disgust. Therefore, if anyone wished to reach the other end of the train, they would climb onto the roof of the "English carriage" and tiptoe, silhouetted by the moon above them, to the next compartment. My father, too, whenever he needed to speak with the driver, climbed out into the night and strolled over the train, clutching a bottle and revolver and greeting passengers in hushed tones who were coming the other way. Fellow officers who were trying to subdue him would never have considered waking up the English. They slept on serenely with their rage for order in the tropics, while the train shunted and reversed into the night and there was chaos and hilarity in the parentheses around them.

Meanwhile, my Uncle Noel, fearful that my father would be charged, was waiting for the train at Kelaniya six miles out of Colombo, quite near where my father had stopped the train to wait for Arthur van Langenberg. So they knew him well there. But the train kept shunting back and forth, never reaching Kelaniya, because at this point my father was absolutely certain the Japanese had mined the train with bombs, which would explode if they reached Colombo. Therefore, anyone who was without a military connection was put off the train at Polgahawela, and he cruised up and down the carriages breaking all the lights that would heat the bombs. He was saving the train and Colombo. While my Uncle Noel waited for over six hours at Kelaniya—the train coming into sight and then retreating once more to the north—my father and two officers under his control searched every piece of luggage. He alone found over twenty-five bombs and as he collected them the others became silent and no longer argued. There were now only fifteen people, save for the sleeping English, on the Trinco-Colombo train, which eventually, as night was ending and the gin ran out, drifted into Kelaniya. My father and the driver had consumed almost seven bottles since that morning.

My Uncle Noel put the bruised John Kotelawala in the back of the Navy jeep he had borrowed. And then my father said he couldn't leave the bombs on the train, they had to take them in the jeep and drop them into the river. He rushed back time and again into the train and brought out the pots of curd that passengers had been carrying. They were carefully loaded into the jeep alongside the prone body of the future Prime Minister. Before my Uncle drove to the hospital, he stopped at the Kelani-Colombo bridge and my father dropped all twenty-five pots into the river below, witnessing huge explosions as they smashed into the water.

My Grandmother died in the blue arms of a jacaranda tree. She could read thunder.

She claimed to have been born outdoors, abruptly, during a picnic, though there is little evidence for this. Her father—who came from a subdued line of Keyts—had thrown caution to the winds and married a Dickman. The bloodline was considered eccentric (one Dickman had set herself on fire) and rumours about the family often percolated across Colombo in hushed tones. "People who married the Dickmans were afraid."

There is no information about Lalla growing up. Perhaps she was a shy child, for those who are magical break from silent structures after years of chrysalis. By the time she was twenty she was living in Colombo and tentatively engaged to Shelton de Saram—a very good-looking and utterly selfish man. He desired the good life, and when Frieda Donhorst arrived from England "with a thin English varnish and the Donhorst checkbook" he promptly married her. Lalla was heartbroken. She went into fits of rage, threw herself on and pounded various beds belonging to her immediate family, and quickly married Willie Gratiaen—a champion cricketer—on the rebound.

Willie was also a broker, and being one of the first Ceylonese to work for the English firm of E. John and Co. brought them most of their local business. The married couple bought a large house called "Palm Lodge" in the heart of Colombo and here, in the three acres that came with the house, they began a dairy. The dairy was Willie's second attempt at raising livestock. Fond of eggs, he had decided earlier to import and raise a breed of black chicken from Australia. At great expense the prize Australorp eggs arrived by ship, ready for hatching, but Lalla accidentally cooked them all while preparing for a dinner party.

Shortly after Willie began the dairy he fell seriously ill. Lalla, unable to cope, would run into neighbours' homes, pound on their beds, and promise to become a Catholic if Willie recovered. He never did and Lalla was left to bring up their two children.

She was not yet thirty, and for the next few years her closest friend was her neighbour, Rene de Saram, who also ran a dairy. Rene's husband disliked Lalla and disliked his wife's chickens. Lalla and the chickens would wake him before dawn every morning, especially Lalla with her loud laughter filtering across the garden as she organized the milkers. One morning Rene woke to silence and, stepping into the garden, discovered her husband tying the beaks of all the chickens with little pieces of string, or in some cases with rubber bands. She protested, but he prevailed and soon they saw their chickens perform a dance of death, dying of exhaustion and hunger, a few managing to escape along Inner Flower Road, some kidnapped by a furious Lalla in the folds of her large brown dress and taken to Palm Lodge where she had them cooked. A year later the husband lapsed into total silence and the only sounds which could be heard from his quarters were barkings and later on the cluck of hens. It is believed he was the victim of someone's charm. For several weeks he clucked, barked, and chirped, tearing his feather pillows into snowstorms, scratching at the expensive parquet floors, leaping from first-storey windows onto the lawn. After he shot himself, Rene was left at the age of thirty-two to bring up their children. So both Rene and Lalla, after years of excessive high living, were to have difficult times—surviving on their wits and character and beauty. Both widows became the focus of the attention of numerous bored husbands. Neither of them was to marry again.

Each had thirty-five cows. Milking began at four-thirty in the morning and by six their milkmen would be cycling all over town to deliver fresh milk to customers. Lalla and Rene took the law into their own hands whenever neces-sary. When one of their cows caught Rinderpest Fever—a disease which could make government officials close down a dairy for months—Rene took the army pistol which had already killed her husband and personally shot it dead. With Lalla's help she burnt it and buried it in her garden. The milk went out that morning as usual, the tin vessels clanking against the handlebars of several bicycles.

Lalla's head milkman at this time was named Brumphy, and when a Scot named McKay made a pass at a servant girl Brumphy stabbed him to death. By the time the police arrived Lalla had hidden him in one of her sheds, and when they came back a second time she had taken Brumphy over to a neighbour named Lillian Bevan. For some reason Mrs. Bevan approved of everything Lalla did. She was sick when Lalla stormed in to hide Brumphy under the bed whose counterpane had wide lace edges that came down to the floor. Lalla explained that it was only a minor crime; when the police came to the Bevan household and described the brutal stabbing in graphic detail Lillian was terrified as the murderer was just a few feet away from her. But she could never disappoint Lalla and kept quiet. The police watched the house for two days and Lillian dutifully halved her meals and passed a share under the bed. "I'm proud of you darling!" said Lalla when she eventually spirited Brumphy away to another location.

However, there was a hearing in court presided over by Judge E. W. Jayawardene—one of Lalla's favourite bridge partners. When she was called to give evidence she kept referring to him as "My Lord My God." E.W. was probably one of the ugliest men in Ceylon at the time. When he asked Lalla if Brumphy was good-looking—trying humorously to suggest some motive for her protecting him—she replied, "Good-looking? Who can say, My Lord My God, some people may find *you* good-looking." She was thrown out of court while the gallery hooted with laughter and gave her a standing ovation. This dialogue is still in the judicial records in the Buller's Road Court Museum. In any case she continued to play bridge with E. W. Jayawardene and their sons would remain close friends.

Apart from rare appearances in court (sometimes to watch other friends give evidence), Lalla's day was carefully planned. She would be up at four with the milkers, oversee the dairy, look after the books, and be finished by 9 a.m. The rest of the day would be given over to gallivanting—social calls, lunch parties, visits from admirers, and bridge. She also brought up her two children. It was in the garden at Palm Lodge that my mother and Dorothy Clementi-Smith would practice their dances, quite often surrounded by cattle.

*

For years Palm Lodge attracted a constant group—first as children, then teenagers, and then young adults. For most of her life children flocked to Lalla, for she was the most casual and irresponsible of chaperones, being far too busy with her own life to oversee them all. Behind Palm Lodge was a paddy field which separated her house from "Royden," where the Daniels lived. When there were complaints that hordes of children ran into Royden with muddy feet, Lalla bought ten pairs of stilts and taught them to walk across the paddy fields on these "boruka-kuls" or "lying legs." Lalla would say "yes" to any request if she was busy at bridge so they knew when to ask her for permission to do the most outrageous things. Every child had to be part of the group. She particularly objected to children being sent for extra tuition on Saturdays and would hire a Wallace Carriage and go searching for children like Peggy Peiris. She swept into the school at noon yelling "PEGGY!!!," fluttering down the halls in her long black clothes loose at the edges like a rooster dragging its tail, and

Peggy's friends would lean over the bannisters and say "Look, look, your mad aunt has arrived."

As these children grew older they discovered that Lalla had very little money. She would take groups out for meals and be refused service as she hadn't paid her previous bills. Everyone went with her anyway, though they could never be sure of eating. It was the same with adults. During one of her grand dinner parties she asked Lionel Wendt who was very shy to carve the meat. A big pot was placed in front of him. As he removed the lid a baby goat jumped out and skittered down the table. Lalla had been so involved with the joke—buying the kid that morning and finding a big enough pot—that she had forgotten about the real dinner and there was nothing to eat once the shock and laughter had subsided.

In the early years her two children, Noel and Doris, could hardly move without being used as part of Lalla's daily theatre. She was constantly dreaming up costumes for my mother to wear to fancy dress parties, which were the rage at the time. Because of Lalla, my mother won every fancy dress competition for three years while in her late teens. Lalla tended to go in for animals or sea creatures. The crowning achievement was my mother's appearance at the Galle Face Dance as a lobster—the outfit bright red and covered with crustaceans and claws which grew out of her shoulder blades and seemed to move of their own accord. The problem was that she could not sit down for the whole evening but had to walk or waltz stiffly from side to side with her various beaux who, although respecting the imagination behind the outfit, found her beautiful frame almost unapproachable. Who knows, this may have been Lalla's ulterior motive. For years my mother tended to be admired from a distance. On the ballroom floor she stood out in her animal or shell fish beauty but claws and caterpillar bulges tended to deflect suitors from thoughts of seduction. When couples paired off to walk along Galle Face Green under the moonlight it would, after all, be embarrassing to be seen escorting a lobster.

When my mother eventually announced her engagement to my father, Lalla turned to friends and said, "What do you *think*, darling, she's going to marry an Ondaatje . . . she's going to marry a *Tamil*!" Years later, when I sent my mother my first book of poems, she met my sister at the door with a shocked face and in exactly the same tone and phrasing said, "What do you *think*, Janet" (her hand holding her cheek to emphasize the tragedy), "Michael has become a *poet*!" Lalla continued to stress the Tamil element in my father's background, which pleased him enormously. For the wedding ceremony she had two marriage chairs decorated in a Hindu style and laughed all through the ceremony. The incident was, however, the beginning of a war with my father.

Eccentrics can be the most irritating people to live with. My mother, for instance, strangely, *never* spoke of Lalla to me. Lalla was loved most by people who saw her arriving from the distance like a storm. She did love children, or at least loved company of any kind—cows, adults, babies, dogs. She always had to be surrounded. But being "grabbed" or "contained" by anyone drove her mad. She would be compassionate to the character of children but tended to avoid holding them on her lap. And she could not abide having grandchildren hold her hands when she took them for walks. She would quickly divert them into the entrance of the frightening maze in the Nuwara Eliya Park and leave them there, lost, while she went off to steal flowers. She was always determined to be physically selfish. Into her sixties she would still complain of how she used to be "pinned down" to breast feed her son before she could leave for dances.

*

With children grown up and out of the way, Lalla busied herself with her sisters and brothers. "Dickie" seemed to be marrying constantly; after David Grenier drowned she married a de Vos, a Wombeck, and then an Englishman. Lalla's brother Vere attempted to remain a bachelor all his life. When she was flirting with Catholicism she decided that Vere should marry her priest's sister—a woman who *had* planned on becoming a nun. The sister also had a dowry of thirty thousand rupees, and both Lalla and Vere were short of money at the time, for both enjoyed expensive drinking sessions. Lalla masterminded the marriage, even though the woman wasn't good-looking and Vere liked good-looking women. On the wedding night the bride prayed for half an hour beside the bed and then started singing hymns, so Vere departed, foregoing nuptial bliss, and for the rest of her life the poor woman had a sign above her door which read "Unloved. Unloved. Unloved." Lalla went to mass the following week, having eaten a huge meal. When refused mass she said, "Then I'll resign," and avoided the church for the rest of her life.

A good many of my relatives from this generation seem to have tormented the church sexually. Italian monks who became enamoured of certain aunts would return to Italy to discard their robes and return to find the women already married. Jesuit fathers too were falling out of the church and into love with the de Sarams with the regularity of mangoes thudding onto dry lawns during a drought. Vere also became the concern of various religious groups that tried to save him. And during the last months of his life he was "held captive" by a group of Roman Catholic nuns in Galle so that no one knew where he was until the announcement of his death.

Vere was known as "a sweet drunk" and he and Lalla always drank together. While Lalla grew loud and cheerful, Vere became excessively courteous. Drink was hazardous for him, however, as he came to believe he escaped the laws of gravity while under the influence. He kept trying to hang his hat on walls where there was no hook and often stepped out of boats to walk home. But drink quietened him except for these few excesses. His close friend, the lawyer Cox Sproule, was a different matter. Cox was charming when sober and brilliant when drunk. He would appear in court stumbling over chairs with a mind clear as a bell, winning cases under a judge who had pleaded with him just that morning not to appear in court in such a condition. He hated the English. Unlike Cox, Vere had no profession to focus whatever talents he had. He did try to become an auctioneer but being both shy and drunk he was a failure. The only job that came his way was supervising Italian prisoners during the war. Once a week he would

ride to Colombo on his motorcycle, bringing as many bottles of alcohol as he could manage for his friends and his
sister. He had encouraged the prisoners to set up a brew-
ery, so that there was a distillery in every hut in the prison
camp. He remained drunk with the prisoners for most of
the war years. Even Cox Sproule joined him for six months
when he was jailed for helping three German spies escape
from the country.

What happened to Lalla's other brother, Evan, no one
knows. But all through her life, when the children sent her
money, Lalla would immediately forward it on to Evan. He
was supposedly a thief and Lalla loved him. "Jesus died to
save sinners," she said, "and I will die for Evan." Evan man-
ages to escape family memory, appearing only now and then
to offer blocs of votes to any friend running for public
office by bringing along all his illegitimate children.

*

By the mid-thirties both Lalla's and Rene's dairies had
been wiped out by Rinderpest. Both were drinking heavily and both were broke.

We now enter the phase when Lalla is best remembered.
Her children were married and out of the way. Most of her
social life had been based at Palm Lodge but now she had
to sell the house, and she burst loose on the country and
her friends like an ancient monarch who had lost all her
possessions. She was free to move wherever she wished, to
do whatever she wanted. She took thorough advantage of
everyone and had bases all over the country. Her schemes
for organizing parties and bridge games exaggerated themselves. She was full of the "passions," whether drunk or

not. She had always loved flowers but in her last decade couldn't be bothered to grow them. Still, whenever she arrived on a visit she would be carrying an armful of flowers and announce, "Darling, I've just been to church and I've stolen some flowers for you. These are from Mrs. Abeysekare's, the lilies are from Mrs. Ratnayake's, the agapanthus is from Violet Meedeniya, and the rest are from *your* garden." She stole flowers compulsively, even in the owner's presence. As she spoke with someone her straying left hand would pull up a prize rose along with the roots, all so that she could appreciate it for that one moment, gaze into it with complete pleasure, swallow its qualities whole, and then hand the flower, discarding it, to the owner. She ravaged some of the best gardens in Colombo and Nuwara Eliya. For some years she was barred from the Hakgalle Public Gardens.

Property was there to be taken or given away. When she was rich she had given parties for all the poor children in the neighbourhood and handed out gifts. When she was poor she still organized them but now would go out to the Pettah market on the morning of the party and steal toys. All her life she had given away everything she owned to whoever wanted it and so now felt free to take whatever she wanted. She was a lyrical socialist. Having no home in her last years, she breezed into houses for weekends or even weeks, cheated at bridge with her closest friends, calling them "damn thieves," "bloody rogues." She only played cards for money and if faced with a difficult contract would throw down her hand, gather the others up, and proclaim "the rest are mine." Everyone knew she was lying but it didn't matter. Once when my brother and two sisters who were very young were playing a game of "beggar-my-neighbour" on the porch, Lalla came to watch. She walked up and down beside them, seemingly very irritated. After ten minutes she could stand it no longer, opened her purse, gave them each two rupees, and said, "Never, *never* play cards for love."

She was in her prime. During the war she opened up a boarding house in Nuwara Eliya with Muriel Potger, a chain smoker who did all the work while Lalla breezed through the rooms saying, "Muriel, for godsake, we can't breathe in this place!"—being more of a pest than a help. If she had to go out she would say, "I'll just freshen up" and disappear into her room for a stiff drink. If there was none she took a quick swig of eau de cologne to snap her awake. Old flames visited her constantly throughout her life. She refused to lose friends; even her first beau, Shelton de Saram, would arrive after breakfast to escort her for walks. His unfortunate wife, Frieda, would always telephone Lalla first and would spend most afternoons riding in her trap through the Cinnamon Gardens or the park searching for them.

Lalla's great claim to fame was that she was the first woman in Ceylon to have a mastectomy. It turned out to be unnecessary but she always claimed to support modern science, throwing herself into new causes. (Even in death her generosity exceeded the physically possible for she had donated her body to six hospitals.) The false breast would never be still for long. She was an energetic person. It would crawl over to join its twin on the right-hand side or sometimes appear on her back, "for dancing" she smirked. She called it her Wandering Jew and would yell at the grandchildren in the middle of a formal dinner to fetch her tit as she had forgotten to put it on. She kept losing the contraption to servants who were mystified by it as well as to the dog, Chindit, who would be found gnawing at the foam as if it were tender chicken. She went through four breasts in her lifetime. One she left on a branch of a tree in Hakgalle Gardens to dry out after a rainstorm, one flew off when she was riding behind Vere on his motorbike, and the third she was very mysterious about, almost embarrassed though Lalla was never embarrassed. Most believed it had been forgotten after a romantic assignation in Trincomalee with a man who may or may not have been in the Cabinet.

*

Children tell little more than animals, said Kipling. When Lalla came to Bishop's College Girls School on Parents' Day and pissed behind bushes—or when in Nuwara Eliya she simply stood with her legs apart and urinated—my sisters were so embarrassed and ashamed they did not admit or speak of this to each other for over fifteen years. Lalla's son Noel was most appalled by her. She, however, was immensely proud of his success, and my Aunt Nedra recalls seeing Lalla sitting on a sack of rice in the fish market surrounded by workers and fishermen, with whom she was having one of her long daily chats, pointing to a picture of a bewigged judge in *The Daily News* and saying in Sinhalese that *this* was *her* son. But Lalla could never be just a mother; that seemed to be only one muscle in her chameleon nature, which had too many other things to reflect. And I am not sure what my mother's relationship was to her. Maybe they were too similar to even recognize much of a problem, both having huge compassionate hearts that never even considered revenge or small-mindedness, both howling and wheezing with laughter over the frailest joke, both carrying their own theatre on their backs. Lalla remained the centre of the world she moved through. She had been beautiful when young but most free after her husband died and her children grew up. There was some sense of divine right she felt she and everyone else had, even if she had to beg for it or steal it. This overbearing charmed flower.

*

In her last years she was searching for the great death. She never found, looking under leaves, the giant snake, the fang which would brush against the ankle like a whisper. A whole generation grew old or died around her. Prime Ministers fell off horses, a jellyfish slid down the throat of a famous swimmer. During the forties she moved with the rest of the country towards Independence and the 20th century. Her freedom accelerated. Her arms still flagged down strange cars for a lift to the Pettah market where she could trade gossip with her friends and place bets in the "bucket shops." She carried everything she really needed with her, and a friend meeting her once at a train station was appalled to be given as a gift a huge fish that Lalla had carried doubled up in her handbag.

She could be silent as a snake or flower. She loved the thunder; it spoke to her like a king. As if her mild dead húsband had been transformed into a cosmic umpire, given the megaphone of nature. Sky noises and the abrupt light told her details of careers, incidental wisdom, allowing her to risk everything because the thunder would warn her along with the snake of lightning. She would stop the car and swim in the Mahaveli, serene among currents, still wearing her hat. Would step out of the river, dry in the sun for five minutes and climb back into the car among the shocked eyeballs of her companions, her huge handbag once more on her lap carrying four packs of cards, possibly a fish.

In August 1947, she received a small inheritance, called her brother Vere, and they drove off to Nuwara Eliya on his motorcycle. She was 68 years old. These were to be her last days. The boarding house she had looked after during the war was empty and so they bought food and booze and moved in to play "Ajoutha"—a card game that normally takes at least eight hours. It was a game the Portuguese had taught the Sinhalese in the 15th century to keep them quiet and preoccupied while they invaded the country. Lalla opened the bottles of Rocklands Gin (the same brand that was destroying her son-in-law) and Vere prepared the Italian menus, which he had learned from his prisoners of war. In her earlier days in Nuwara Eliya, Lalla would have been up at dawn to walk through the park—inhabited at that hour only by nuns and monkeys—walk round the golf-course where gardeners would stagger under the weight of giant python-like hoses as they watered the greens. But now she slept till noon, and in the early evening rode up to Moon Plains, her arms spread out like a crucifix behind Vere.

Moon Plains. Drowned in blue and gold flowers whose names she had never bothered to learn, tugged by the wind, leaning in angles for miles and miles against the hills 5,000 feet above sea level. They watched the exit of the sun and the sudden appearance of the moon half way up the sky. Those lovely accidental moons—a horn a chalice a thumbnail—and then they would climb onto the motorcycle, the 60-year-old brother and the 68-year-old sister, who was his best friend forever.

Riding back on August 13, 1947, they heard the wild thunder and she knew someone was going to die. Death, however, not to be read out there. She gazed and listened but there seemed to be no victim or parabola end beyond her. It rained hard during the last mile to the house and they went indoors to drink for the rest of the evening. The next day the rains continued and she refused Vere's offer of a ride knowing there would be death soon. "Cannot wreck this perfect body, Vere. The police will spend hours searching for my breast thinking it was lost in the crash." So they played two-handed Ajoutha and drank. But now she could not sleep at all, and they talked as they never had about husbands, lovers, his various possible marriages. She did not mention her readings of the thunder to Vere, who was now almost comatose on the bluebird print sofa. But she could not keep her eyes closed like him and at 5 a.m. on August 15, 1947, she wanted fresh air, needed to walk, a walk to Moon Plains, no motorcycle, no danger, and she stepped out towards the still dark night of almost dawn and straight into the floods.

For two days and nights they had been oblivious to the

amount of destruction outside their home. The whole
country was mauled by the rains that year. Ratmalana,
Bentota, Chilaw, Anuradhapura, were all under water. The
forty-foot-high Peredeniya Bridge had been swept away. In
Nuwara Eliya, Galways's Land Bird Sanctuary and the Golf
Course were ten feet under water. Snakes and fish from the
lake swam into the windows of the Golf Club, into the
bar, and around the indoor badminton court. Fish were
found captured in the badminton nets when the flood re-
ceded a week later. Lalla took one step off the front porch
and was immediately hauled away by an arm of water, her
handbag bursting open. 208 cards moved ahead of her like
a disturbed nest as she was thrown downhill still comfortable and drunk, snagged for a few moments on the railings
of the Good Shepherd Convent and then lifted away
towards the town of Nuwara Eliya.

It was her last perfect journey. The new river in the
street moved her right across the race course and park
towards the bus station. As the light came up slowly she
was being swirled fast, "floating" (as ever confident of surviving this too) alongside branches and leaves, the dawn
starting to hit flamboyant trees as she slipped past them like
a dark log, shoes lost, false breast lost. She was free as a fish,
traveling faster than she had in years, fast as Vere's motorcycle, only now there was this *roar* around her. She over-
took Jesus lizards that swam and ran in bursts over the
water, she was surrounded by tired half-drowned fly-
catchers screaming *tack tack tack tack*, frogmouths, nightjars
forced to keep awake, brain-fever birds and their irritating
ascending scales, snake eagles, scimitar-babblers, they rode

the air around Lalla wishing to perch on her unable to alight on anything except what was moving.

What was moving was rushing flood. In the park she floated over the intricate fir tree hedges of the maze—which would always continue to terrify her grandchildren—its secret spread out naked as a skeleton for her. The symmetrical flower beds also began to receive the day's light and Lalla gazed down at them with wonder, moving as lazily as that long dark scarf which trailed off her neck brushing the branches and never catching. She would always wear silk, as she showed us, her grandchildren, would pull the scarf like a fluid through the ring removed from her finger, pulled sleepily through, as she moved now, awake to the new angle of her favourite trees, the Syzygium, the Araucaria Pine, over the now unnecessary iron gates of the park, and through the town of Nuwara Eliya itself and its shops and stalls where she had haggled for guavas, now six feet under water, windows smashed in by the weight of all this collected rain.

Drifting slower she tried to hold onto things. A bicycle hit her across the knees. She saw the dead body of a human. She began to see the drowned dogs of the town. Cattle. She saw men on roofs fighting with each other, looting, almost surprised by the quick dawn in the mountains revealing them, not even watching her magic ride, the alcohol still in her—serene and relaxed.

Below the main street of Nuwara Eliya the land drops suddenly and Lalla fell into deeper waters, past the houses of "Cranleigh" and "Ferncliff." They were homes she knew well, where she had played and argued over cards. The water here was rougher and she went under for longer and longer moments coming up with a gasp and then pulled down like bait, pulled under by something not comfortable any more, and then there was the great blue ahead of her, like a sheaf of blue wheat, like a large eye that peered towards her, and she hit it and was dead.

Photograph

My Aunt pulls out the album and there is the photograph I have been waiting for all my life. My father and mother together. May 1932.

They are on their honeymoon and the two of them, very soberly dressed, have walked into a photographic studio. The photographer is used to wedding pictures. He has probably seen every pose. My father sits facing the camera, my mother stands beside him and bends over so that her face is in profile on a level with his. Then they both begin to make hideous faces.

My father's pupils droop to the south-west corner of his sockets. His jaw falls and resettles into a groan that is half idiot, half shock. (All this emphasized by his dark suit and well-combed hair.) My mother in white has twisted her lovely features and stuck out her jaw and upper lip so that her profile is in the posture of a monkey. The print is made into a postcard and sent through the mails to various friends. On the back my father has written *"What we think of married life."*

Everything is there, of course. Their good looks behind

the tortured faces, their mutual humour, and the fact that both of them are hams of a very superior sort. The evidence I wanted that they were absolutely perfect for each other. My father's tanned skin, my mother's milk paleness, and this theatre of their own making.

It is the only photograph I have found of the two of them together.

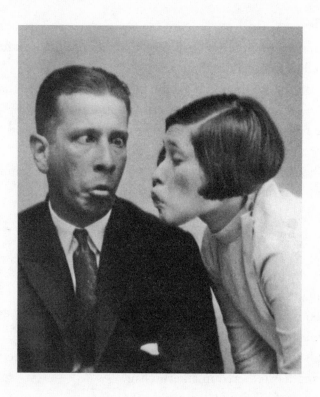

LIGHT

for Doris Gratiaen

Midnight storm. Trees walking off across the fields in fury
naked in the spark of lightning.
I sit on the white porch on the brown hanging cane chair
coffee in my hand midnight storm midsummer night.
The past, friends and family, drift into the rain shower.
Those relatives in my favourite slides
re-shot from old minute photographs so they now stand
complex ambiguous grainy on my wall.

This is my Uncle who turned up for his marriage
on an elephant. He was a chaplain.
This shy looking man in the light jacket and tie was
    infamous,
when he went drinking he took the long blonde beautiful
    hair
of his wife and put one end in the cupboard and locked it
leaving her tethered in an armchair.
He was terrified of her possible adultery
and this way died peaceful happy to the end.
My Grandmother, who went to a dance in a muslin dress

with fireflies captured and embedded in the cloth, shining
and witty. This calm beautiful face
organized wild acts in the tropics.
She hid the milkman in her house
after he had committed murder and at the trial
was thrown out of the court for making jokes at the
   judge.
Her son became a Q.C.
This is my brother at 6. With his cousin and his sister
and Pam de Voss who fell on a penknife and lost her eye.
My Aunt Christie. She knew Harold Macmillan was a spy
communicating with her through pictures in the news-
   papers.
Every picture she believed asked her to forgive him,
his hound eyes pleading.

Her husband, Uncle Fitzroy, a doctor in Ceylon,
had a memory sharp as scalpels into his 80's,
though I never bothered to ask him about anything
—interested then more in the latest recordings of Bobby
   Darin.

And this is my Mother with her brother Noel in fancy
   dress.
They are 7 and 8 years old, a hand-coloured photograph,
it is the earliest picture I have. The one I love most.
A picture of my kids at Halloween
has the same contact and laughter.
My Uncle dying at 68, and my Mother a year later dying
   at 68.

She told me about his death and the day he died
his eyes clearing out of illness as if seeing
right through the room the hospital and she said
he saw something so clear and good his whole body
for a moment became youthful and she remembered
when she sewed badges on his trackshirts.
Her voice joyous in telling me this, her face light and
    clear.
(My firefly Grandmother also dying at 68.)

These are the fragments I have of them, tonight
in this storm, the dogs restless on the porch.
They were all laughing, crazy, and vivid in their prime.
At a party my drunk Father
tried to explain a complex operation on chickens
and managed to kill them all in the process, the guests
having dinner an hour later while my Father slept
and the kids watched the servants clean up the litter
of beaks and feathers on the lawn.

These are their fragments, all I remember,
wanting more knowledge of them. In the mirror and in
    my kids
I see them in my flesh. Wherever we are
they parade in my brain and the expanding stories
connect to the grey grainy pictures on the wall,
as they hold their drinks or 20 years later
hold grandchildren, pose with favourite dogs,
coming through the light, the electricity, which the storm
destroyed an hour ago, a tree going down by the highway

so that now inside the kids play dominoes by candlelight
and out here the thick rain static the spark of my match

                                        to a cigarette

and the trees across the fields leaving me, distinct
lonely in their own knife scars and cow-chewed bark
frozen in the jagged light as if snapped in their run
the branch arms waving to what was a second ago the
    dark sky
when in truth like me they haven't moved.
Haven't moved an inch from me.

CLAUDE GLASS

He is told about
the previous evening's behaviour.

Starting with a punchbowl
on the volleyball court.
Dancing and falling across coffee tables,
asking his son Are *you* the bastard
who keeps telling me I'm drunk?
kissing the limbs of women
suspicious of his friends serenading
five pigs by the barn
heaving a wine glass towards garden
and continually going through gates
into the dark fields
and collapsing.
His wife half carrying him home
rescuing him from departing cars,
complains this morning
of a sore shoulder.
                          And even later

his thirteen-year-old daughter's struggle
to lift him into the back kitchen
after he has passed out, resting his head on rocks,
wondering what he was looking for in dark fields.

For he has always loved that ancient darkness
where the flat rocks glide like Japanese tables
where he can remove clothes
and lie with moonlight on the day's heat
hardened in stone, drowning
in this star blanket this sky
like a giant trout
conscious how the heaven
careens over him
as he moves in back fields
kissing the limbs of trees
or placing ear on stone which rocks him
and then stands to watch the house
in its oasis of light.
And he knows something is happening there to him
solitary while he spreads his arms
and holds everything that is slipping away together.

He is suddenly in the heat of the party
slouching towards women, revolving
round one unhappy shadow.
That friend who said he would find
the darkest place, and then wave.
He is not a lost drunk
like his father or his friend, can,

he says, stop on a dime, and he can
he could because even now, now in
this brilliant darkness where
grass has lost its colour and it's all
fucking Yeats and moonlight, he knows
this colourless grass is making his bare feet green
for it is the hour of magic
which no matter what sadness
leaves him grinning.
At certain hours of the night
ducks are nothing but landscape
just voices breaking as they nightmare.
The weasel wears their blood
home like a scarf,
cows drain over the horizon
                              and the dark
vegetables hum onward underground

but the mouth
        wants plum.

Moves from room to room
where brown beer glass
smashed lounges at his feet
opens the long rust stained gate
and steps towards invisible fields
that he knows from years of daylight.
He snorts in the breeze
which carries a smell
of cattle on its back.

What this place does not have
is the white paint of bathing cabins
the leak of eucalyptus.
During a full moon
outcrops of rock shine
skunks spray abstract into the air
cows burp as if practicing
the name of Francis Ponge.
His drunk state wants the mesh of place.
Ludwig of Bavaria's Roof Garden—
glass plants, iron parrots
Venus Grottos, tarpaulins of Himalaya.
By the kitchen sink he tells someone
from now on I will drink only landscapes
—here, pour me a cup of Spain.

Opens the gate and stumbles
blood like a cassette through the body
away from the lights, unbuttoning,
this desire to be riverman.

Tentatively
        he recalls
his drunk invitation to the river.
He has steered the awesome car
past sugarbush to the blue night water
and steps out
speaking to branches
and the gulp of toads.

Subtle applause of animals.
A snake leaves a path
like temporary fossil.
                    He falls
back onto the intricacies
of gearshift and steering wheel
alive as his left arm
which now departs out of the window
trying to tug passing sumac
pine   bush   tamarack
into the car
                    to the party.
Drunkenness opens his arms like a gate
and over the car invisible insects
ascend out of the beams like meteorite
crushed dust of the moon
. . . he waits for the magic star called Lorca.

On the front lawn a sheet
tacked across a horizontal branch.
A projector starts a parade
of journeys, landscapes, relatives,
friends leaping out within pebbles of water
caught by the machine as if creating rain.

Later when wind frees the sheet
and it collapses like powder in the grass
pictures fly without target
and howl their colours over Southern Ontario
clothing burdock

rhubarb a floating duck.
Landscapes and stories
flung into branches
and the dog walks under the hover of the swing
beam of the projection bursting in his left eye.

The falling sheet the star of Lorca swoops
someone gets up and heaves his glass
into the vegetable patch
towards the slow stupid career of beans.

This is the hour
when dead men sit
and write each other.
       "Concerning the words we never said
       during morning hours of the party
       there was glass under my bare feet
       laws of the kitchen were broken
       and each word moved
       in my mouth like muscle . . ."

This is the hour for sudden journeying.
             Cervantes accepts
a 17th Century invitation
from the Chinese Emperor.
Schools of Chinese-Spanish Linguistics!
Rivers of the world meet!
And here
ducks dressed in Asia
pivot on foreign waters.

At 4 a.m. he wakes in the sheet
that earlier held tropics in its whiteness.
The invited river flows through the house
into the kitchen up
stairs, he awakens and moves within it.
In the dim light
he sees the turkish carpet under water,
low stools, glint
of piano pedals, even a sleeping dog
whose dreams may be of rain.

It is a river he has walked elsewhere
now visiting moving with him at the hip
to kitchen where a friend sleeps in a chair
head on the table his grip
still round a glass, legs underwater.

He wants to relax
and give in to the night
fall horizontal and swim
to the back kitchen where his daughter sleeps.
He wishes to swim
to each of his family and gaze
at their underwater dreaming
this magic chain of bubbles.
Wife, son, household guests, all
comfortable in clean river water.

He is aware that for hours
there has been no conversation,
tongues have slid to stupidity on alcohol
sleeping mouths are photographs of yells.

He stands waiting, the sentinel,
shambling back and forth, his anger
and desire against the dark
which, if he closes his eyes,
will lose them all.

                  The oven light
shines up through water at him
a bathysphere   a ghost ship
and in the half drowned room
the crickets like small pins
begin to tack down
the black canvas of this night,
begin to talk their hesitant
gnarled epigrams to each other
across the room.
                Creak and echo.
Creak and echo. With absolute clarity
he knows where he is.

THE CINNAMON PEELER

If I were a cinnamon peeler
I would ride your bed
and leave the yellow bark dust
on your pillow.

Your breasts and shoulders would reek
you could never walk through markets
without the profession of my fingers
floating over you. The blind would
stumble certain of whom they approached
though you might bathe
under rain gutters, monsoon.

Here on the upper thigh
at this smooth pasture
neighbour to your hair
or the crease
that cuts your back. This ankle.
You will be known among strangers
as the cinnamon peeler's wife.

I could hardly glance at you
before marriage
never touch you
—your keen nosed mother, your rough brothers.
I buried my hands
in saffron, disguised them
over smoking tar,
helped the honey gatherers . . .

When we swam once
I touched you in water
and our bodies remained free,
you could hold me and be blind of smell.
You climbed the bank and said

        this is how you touch other women
the grass cutter's wife, the lime burner's daughter.
And you searched your arms
for the missing perfume

                    and knew

        what good is it
to be the lime burner's daughter
left with no trace
as if not spoken to in the act of love
as if wounded without the pleasure of a scar.

You touched
your belly to my hands
in the dry air and said
I am the cinnamon
peeler's wife. Smell me.

The Bridge

from IN THE SKIN OF A LION

A truck carries fire at five a.m. through central Toronto, along Dundas Street and up Parliament Street, moving north. Aboard the flatbed three men stare into passing darkness—their muscles relaxed in this last half-hour before work—as if they don't own the legs or the arms jostling against their bodies and the backboard of the Ford.

Written in yellow over the green door is DOMINION BRIDGE COMPANY. But for now all that is visible is the fire on the flatbed burning over the three-foot by three-foot metal dish, cooking the tar in a cauldron, leaving this odour on the streets for anyone who would step out into the early morning and swallow the air.

The truck rolls burly under the arching trees, pauses at certain intersections where more workers jump onto the flatbed, and soon there are eight men, the fire crackling, hot tar now and then spitting onto the back of a neck or an ear. Soon there are twenty, crowded and silent.

The light begins to come out of the earth. They see their hands, the textures on a coat, the trees they had known were there. At the top of Parliament Street the truck turns east, passes the Rosedale fill, and moves towards the half-built viaduct.

The men jump off. The unfinished road is full of ruts and the fire and the lights of the truck bounce, the suspension wheezing. The truck travels so slowly the men are walking faster, in the cold dawn air, even though it is summer.

Later they will remove coats and sweaters, then by eleven their shirts, bending over the black rivers of tar in just their trousers, boots, and caps. But now the thin layer of frost is everywhere, coating the machines and cables, brittle on the rain puddles they step through. The fast evaporation of darkness. As light emerges they see their breath, the clarity of the air being breathed out of them. The truck finally stops at the edge of the viaduct, and its lights are turned off.

The bridge goes up in a dream. It will link the east end with the centre of the city. It will carry traffic, water, and electricity across the Don Valley. It will carry trains that have not even been invented yet.

Night and day. Fall light. Snow light. They are always working—horses and wagons and men arriving for work on the Danforth side at the far end of the valley.

There are over 4,000 photographs from various angles of the bridge in its time-lapse evolution. The piers sink into bedrock fifty feet below the surface through clay and shale and quicksand—45,000 cubic yards of earth are excavated. The network of scaffolding stretches up.

Men in a maze of wooden planks climb deep into the

shattered light of blond wood. A man is an extension of hammer, drill, flame. Drill smoke in his hair. A cap falls into the valley, gloves are buried in stone dust.

Then the new men arrive, the "electricals," laying grids of wire across the five arches, carrying the exotic three-bowl lights, and on October 18, 1918, it is completed. Lounging in mid-air.

The bridge. The bridge. Christened "Prince Edward." The Bloor Street Viaduct.

During the political ceremonies a figure escaped by bicycle through the police barriers. The first member of the public. Not the expected show car containing officials, but this one anonymous and cycling like hell to the east end of the city. In the photographs he is a blur of intent. He wants the virginity of it, the luxury of such space. He circles twice, the string of onions that he carries on his shoulder splaying out, and continues.

But he was not the first. The previous midnight the workers had arrived and brushed away officials who guarded the bridge in preparation for the ceremonies the next day, moved with their own flickering lights—their candles for the bridge dead—like a wave of civilization, a net of summer insects over the valley.

And the cyclist too on his flight claimed the bridge in that blurred movement, alone and illegal. Thunderous applause greeted him at the far end.

On the west side of the bridge is Bloor Street, on the east side is Danforth Avenue. Originally cart roads, mud roads, planked in 1910, they are now being tarred. Bricks are banged into the earth and narrow creeks of sand are poured in between them. The tar is spread. *Bitumiers, bitumatori,* tarrers, get onto their knees and lean their weight over the wooden block irons, which arc and sweep. The smell of tar seeps through the porous body of their clothes. The black of it is permanent under the nails. They can feel the bricks under their kneecaps as they crawl backwards towards the bridge, their bodies almost horizontal over the viscous black river, their heads drunk within the fumes.

Hey, Caravaggio!

The young man gets up off his knees and looks back into the sun. He walks to the foreman, lets go of the two wooden blocks he is holding so they hang by the leather thongs from his belt, bouncing against his knees as he walks. Each man carries the necessities of his trade with him. When Caravaggio quits a year later he will cut the thongs with a fish knife and fling the blocks into the half-dry tar. Now he walks back in a temper and gets down on his knees again. Another fight with the foreman.

All day they lean over tar, over the twenty yards of black river that has been spread since morning. It glistens and eases in sunlight. Schoolkids grab bits of tar and chew them, first cooling the pieces in their hands, then popping them into their mouths. It concentrates the saliva for spitting contests. The men plunk cans of beans into the blackness to heat them up for their lunch.

In winter, snow removes the scent of tar, the scent of pitched cut wood. The Don River floods below the unfinished bridge, ice banging at the feet of the recently built piers. On winter mornings men fan out nervous over the whiteness. Where does the earth end? There are flares along the edge of the bridge on winter nights—worst shift of all—where they hammer the nails in through snow. The bridge builders balance on a strut, the flares wavering behind them, aiming their hammers towards the noise of a nail they cannot see.

*

The last thing Rowland Harris, Commissioner of Public Works, would do in the evenings during its construction was have himself driven to the edge of the viaduct, to sit for a while. At midnight the half-built bridge over the valley seemed deserted—just lanterns tracing its outlines. But there was always a night shift of thirty or forty men. After a while Harris removed himself from the car, lit a cigar, and walked onto the bridge. He loved this viaduct. It was his first child as head of Public Works, much of it planned before he took over but he had bullied it through. It was Harris who envisioned that it could carry not just cars but trains on a lower trestle. It could also transport water from the east-end plants to the centre of the city. Water was Harris' great passion. He wanted giant water mains travelling across the valley as part of the viaduct.

He slipped past the barrier and walked towards the working men. Few of them spoke English but they knew who he was. Sometimes he was accompanied by Pomphrey, an architect, the strange one from England who was later to design for Commissioner Harris one of the city's grandest buildings—the water filtration plant in the east end.

For Harris the night allowed scope. Night removed the limitations of detail and concentrated on form. Harris would bring Pomphrey with him, past the barrier, onto the first stage of the bridge that ended sixty yards out in the air. The wind moved like something ancient against them. All men on the bridge had to buckle on halter ropes. Harris spoke of his plans to this five-foot-tall Englishman, struggling his way into Pomphrey's brain. Before the real city could be seen it had to be imagined, the way rumours and tall tales were a kind of charting.

One night they had driven there at eleven o'clock, crossed the barrier, and attached themselves once again to the rope harnesses. This allowed them to stand near the edge to study the progress of the piers and the steel arches. There was a fire on the bridge where the night workers congregated, flinging logs and other remnants onto it every so often, warming themselves before they walked back and climbed over the edge of the bridge into the night.

They were working on a wood-facing for the next pier so that concrete could be poured in. As they sawed and hammered, wind shook the light from the flares attached to the side of the abutment. Above them, on the deck of the bridge, builders were carrying huge Ingersoll-Rand air compressors and cables.

An April night in 1917. Harris and Pomphrey were on the bridge, in the dark wind. Pomphrey had turned west and was suddenly stilled. His hand reached out to touch

Harris on the shoulder, a gesture he had never made before.

—Look!

Walking on the bridge were five nuns.

Past the Dominion Steel castings wind attacked the body directly. The nuns were walking past the first group of workers at the fire. The bus, Harris thought, must have dropped them off near Castle Frank and the nuns had, with some confusion at that hour, walked the wrong way in the darkness.

They had passed the black car under the trees and talking cheerfully stepped past the barrier into a landscape they did not know existed—onto a tentative carpet over the piers, among the night labourers. They saw the fire and the men. A few tried to wave them back. There was a mule attached to a wagon. The hiss and jump of machines made the ground under them lurch. A smell of creosote. One man was washing his face in a barrel of water.

The nuns were moving towards a thirty-yard point on the bridge when the wind began to scatter them. They were thrown against the cement mixers and steam shovels, careering from side to side, in danger of going over the edge.

Some of the men grabbed and enclosed them, pulling leather straps over their shoulders, but two were still loose. Harris and Pomphrey at the far end looked on helplessly as one nun was lifted up and flung against the compressors. She stood up shakily and then the wind jerked her sideways, scraping her along the concrete and right off the edge of the bridge. She disappeared into the night by the third abutment, into the long depth of air which held nothing, only sometimes a rivet or a dropped hammer during the day.

Then there was no longer any fear on the bridge. The worst, the incredible, had happened. A nun had fallen off the Prince Edward Viaduct before it was even finished. The men covered in wood shavings or granite dust held the women against them. And Commissioner Harris at the far end stared along the mad pathway. This was his first child and it had already become a murderer.

The man in mid-air under the central arch saw the shape fall towards him, in that second knowing his rope would not hold them both. He reached to catch the figure while his other hand grabbed the metal pipe edge above him to lessen the sudden jerk on the rope. The new weight ripped the arm that held the pipe out of its socket and he screamed, so whoever might have heard him up there would have thought the scream was from the falling figure. The halter thulked, jerking his chest up to his throat. The right arm was all agony now—but his hand's timing had been immaculate, the grace of the habit, and he found himself a moment later holding the figure against him dearly.

He saw it was a black-garbed bird, a girl's white face. He saw this in the light that sprayed down inconstantly from a flare fifteen yards above them. They hung in the halter, pivoting over the valley, his broken arm loose on one side of him, holding the woman with the other. Her body was in shock, her huge eyes staring into the face of Nicholas Temelcoff.

Scream, please, Lady, he whispered, the pain terrible. He asked her to hold him by the shoulders, to take the weight off his one good arm. A sway in the wind. She could not speak though her eyes glared at him bright, just staring at him. *Scream, please*. But she could not.

During the night, the long chutes through which wet concrete slid were unused and hung loose so the open spouts wavered a few feet from the valley floor. The tops of these were about ten feet from him now. He knew this without seeing them, even though they fell outside the scope of light. If they attempted to slide the chute their weight would make it vertical and dangerous. They would have to go further—to reach the lower-deck level of the bridge where there were structures built for possible water mains.

We have to swing. She had her hands around his shoulders now, the wind assaulting them. The two strangers were in each other's arms, beginning to swing wilder, once more, past the lip of the chute which had tempted them, till they were almost at the lower level of the rafters. He had his one good arm free. Saving her now would be her responsibility.

She was in shock, her face bright when they reached the lower level, like a woman with a fever. She was in no shape to be witnessed, her veil loose, her cropped hair open to the long wind down the valley. Once they reached the cat-walk she saved him from falling back into space. He was exhausted. She held him and walked with him like a lover along the unlit lower parapet towards the west end of the bridge.

Above them the others stood around the one fire, talking agitatedly. The women were still tethered to the men and not looking towards the stone edge where she had gone over, falling in darkness. The one with that small scar against her nose . . . she was always falling into windows, against chairs. She was always unlucky.

The Commissioner's chauffeur slept in his car as Temelcoff and the nun walked past, back on real earth away from the bridge. Before they reached Parliament Street they cut south through the cemetery. He seemed about to faint and she held him against a gravestone. She forced him to hold his arm rigid, his fist clenched. She put her hands underneath it like a stirrup and jerked upwards so he screamed out again, her whole body pushing up with all of her strength, groaning as if about to lift him and then holding him, clutching him tight. She had seen the sweat jump out of his face. *Get me a shot. Get me.* . . . She removed her veil and wrapped the arm tight against his side. *Parliament and Dundas . . . few more blocks.* So she went down Parliament Street with him. Where she was going she didn't know. On Eastern Avenue she knocked at the door he pointed to. All these abrupt requests—scream, swing, knock, get me. Then a man opened the door and let them into the Ohrida Lake Restaurant. *Thank you, Kosta. Go back to bed, I'll lock it.* And the man, the friend, walked back upstairs.

She stood in the middle of the restaurant in darkness. The chairs and tables were pushed back to the edge of the room. Temelcoff brought out a bottle of brandy from under the counter and picked up two small glasses in the fingers of the same hand. He guided her to a small table, then walked back and, with a switch behind the zinc counter, turned on a light near her table. There were crests on the wall.

She still hadn't said a word. He remembered she had not even screamed when she fell. That had been him.

*

Nicholas Temelcoff is famous on the bridge, a daredevil. He is given all the difficult jobs and he takes them. He descends into the air with no fear. He is a solitary. He assembles ropes, brushes the tackle and pulley at his waist, and falls off the bridge like a diver over the edge of a boat. The rope roars alongside him, slowing with the pressure of his half-gloved hands. He is burly on the ground and then falls with terrific speed, grace, using the wind to push himself into corners of abutments so he can check driven rivets, sheering valves, the drying of the concrete under bearing plates and padstones. He stands in the air banging the crown pin into the upper cord and then shepherds the lower cord's slip-joint into position. Even in archive photographs it is difficult to find him. Again and again you see vista before you and the eye must search along the wall of sky to the speck of burned paper across the valley that is him, an exclamation mark, somewhere in the distance between bridge and river. He floats at the three hinges of the crescent-shaped steel arches. These knit the bridge together. The moment of cubism.

He is happiest at daily chores—ferrying tools from pier

down to trestle, or lumber that he pushes in the air before him as if swimming in a river. He is a spinner. He links everyone. He meets them as they cling—braced by wind against the metal they are riveting or the wood sheeting they hammer into—but he has none of their fear. Always he carries his own tackle, hunched under his ropes and dragging the shining pitons behind him. He sits on a coiled seat of rope while he eats his lunch on the bridge. If he finishes early he cycles down Parliament Street to the Ohrida Lake Restaurant and sits in the darkness of the room as if he has had enough of light. Enough of space.

His work is so exceptional and time-saving he earns one dollar an hour while the other bridge workers receive forty cents. There is no jealousy towards him. No one dreams of doing half the things he does. For night work he is paid $1.25, swinging up into the rafters of a trestle holding a flare, free-falling like a dead star. He does not really need to see things, he has charted all that space, knows the pier footings, the width of the crosswalks in terms of seconds of movement—281 feet and 6 inches make up the central span of the bridge. Two flanking spans of 240 feet, two end spans of 158 feet. He slips into openings on the lower deck, tackles himself up to bridge level. He knows the precise height he is over the river, how long his ropes are, how many seconds he can free-fall to the pulley. It does not matter if it is day or night, he could be blindfolded. Black space is time. After swinging for three seconds he puts his feet up to link with the concrete edge of the next pier. He knows his position in the air as if he is mercury slipping across a map.

*

A South River parrot hung in its cage by the doorway of the Ohrida Lake Restaurant, too curious and interested in the events of the night to allow itself to be blanketed. It watched the woman who stood dead centre in the room in darkness. The man turned on one light behind the counter. Nicholas Temelcoff came over to the bird for a moment's visit after getting the drinks. "Well, Alicia, my heart, how are you?" And walked away not waiting for the bird's reply, the fingers of his left hand delicately holding the glasses, his arm cradling the bottle.

He muttered as if continuing his conversation with the bird, in the large empty room. From noon till two it was full of men, eating and drinking. Kosta the owner and his waiter performing raucous shows for the crowd—the boss yelling insults at the waiter, chasing him past customers. Nicholas remembered the first time he had come there. The dark coats of men, the arguments of Europe.

He poured a brandy and pushed it over to her. "You don't have to drink this but you can if you wish. Or see it as a courtesy." He drank quickly and poured himself another. "Thank you," he said, touching his arm curiously as if it were the arm of a stranger.

She shook her head to communicate it was not all right, that it needed attention.

"Yes, but not now. Now I want to sit here." There was a silence between them. "Just to drink and talk quietly. . . . It is always night here. People step in out of sunlight and must move slow in the darkness."

He drank again. "Just for the pain." She smiled. "Now

music." He stood up free of the table as he spoke and went behind the counter and turned the wireless on low. He spun the dial till there was bandstand. He sat down again opposite her. "Lot of pain. But I feel good." He leaned back in his chair, holding up his glass. "Alive." She picked up her glass and drank.

"Where did you get that scar?" He pointed his thumb to the side of her nose. She pulled back.

"Don't be shy . . . talk. You must talk." He wanted her to come out to him, even in anger, though he didn't want anger. Feeling such ease in the Ohrida Lake Restaurant, feeling the struts of the chair along his back, her veil tight on his arm. He just wanted her there near him, night all around them, where he could look after her, bring her out of the shock with some grace.

"I got about twenty scars," he said, "all over me. One on my ear here." He turned and leaned forward so the wall-light fell onto the side of his head. "See? Also this under my chin, that also broke my jaw. A coiling wire did that. Nearly kill me, broke my jaw. Lots more. My knees. . . ." He talked on. Hot tar burns on his arm. Nails in his calves. Drinking up, pouring her another shot, the woman's song on the radio. She heard the lyrics underneath Temelcoff's monologue as he talked and half mouthed the song and searched into her bright face. Like a woman with a fever.

This is the first time she has sat in a Macedonian bar, in any bar, with a drinking man. There is a faint glow from the varnished tables, the red checkered tablecloths of the day are folded and stacked. The alcove with its serving counter has an awning hanging over it. She realizes the darkness represents a Macedonian night where customers sit outside at their tables. Light can come only from the bar, the stars, the clock dressed in its orange and red electricity. So when customers step in at any time, what they are entering is an old courtyard of the Balkans. A violin. Olive trees. Permanent evening. Now the arbour-like wallpaper makes sense to her. Now the parrot has a language.

He talked on, slipping into phrases from the radio songs which is how he learned his words and pronunciations. He talked about himself, tired, unaware his voice split now into two languages, the woman hearing everything he said and trying to remember it all. He could see her eyes were alive, interpreting the room. He noticed the almost-tap of her finger to the radio music.

The blue eyes stayed on him as he moved, leaning his head against the wall. He drank, his breath deep into the glass so the fumes would hit his eyes and the sting of it keep him awake. Then he looked back at her. How old was she? Her brown hair so short, so new to the air. He wanted to coast his hand through it.

"I love your hair," he said. "Thank you . . . for the help. For taking the drink."

She leaned forward earnestly and looked at him, searching out his face now. Words just on the far side of her skin, about to fall out. Wanting to know his name which he had forgotten to tell her. "I love your hair." His shoulder was against the wall and he was trying to look up. Then his eyes were closed. So deeply asleep he would be gone for hours.

She could twist him around like a puppet and he wouldn't waken.

She felt as if she were the only one alive in this building. In such formal darkness. There was a terrible taste from that one drink still on her tongue, so she walked behind the zinc counter, turning on the tap to wash out her mouth. She moved the dial of the radio around a bit but brought it back securely to the same station. She was looking for that song he had half-sung along with earlier, the voice of the singer strangely powerful and lethargic. She saw herself in the mirror. A woman whose hair was showing, caught illicit. She did what he had wanted to do. She ran her hand over her hair briefly. Then turned from her image.

Leaning forward, she laid her face on the cold zinc, the chill there even past midnight. Upon her cheek, her eyelid. She let her skull roll to cool her forehead. The zinc was an edge of another country. She put her ear against the grey ocean of it. Its memory of a day's glasses. The spill and the wiping cloth. Confessional. Tabula Rasa.

At the table she positioned the man comfortably so he would not fall on his arm. *What is your name?* she whispered. She bent down and kissed him, then began walking around the room. This orchard. Strangers kiss softly as moths, she thought.

*

In certain weather, when fog fills the valley, the men stay close to each other. They arrive for work and walk onto a path that disappears into whiteness. What country exists on the other side? They move in groups of three or four. Many have already died during the building of the bridge. But especially on mornings like this there is a prehistoric fear, a giant bird lifting one of the men into the air. . . .

Nicholas has removed his hat, stepped into his harness, and dropped himself off the edge, falling thirty feet down through fog. He hangs under the spine of the bridge. He can see nothing, just his hands and the yard of pulley-rope above him. Six in the morning and he's already lost to that community of men on the bridge who are also part of the fairy tale.

He is parallel to the lattice-work of hanging structures. Now he enters the cages of steel and wood like a diver entering a sunken vessel that could at any moment tip over into deeper fracture zones of the sea floor. Nicholas Temelcoff works as the guy derricks raise and lower the steel—assembling it further out towards the next pier. He directs the steel through the fog. He is a fragment at the end of the steel bone the derrick carries on the end of its sixty-foot boom. The steel and Nicholas are raised up to a temporary track and from there the "travellers" handle it. On the west end of the viaduct a traveller is used to erect the entire 150-foot span. The travellers are twin derricks fitted with lattice-work booms that can lift twelve tons into any position, like a carrot off the nose of the most recently built section of the bridge.

Nicholas is not attached to the travellers, his rope and pulleys link up only with the permanent steel of a completed section of the bridge. Travellers have collapsed twice before this and fallen to the floor of the valley. He is not attaching himself to a falling structure. But he hangs beside it, in the blind whiteness, slipping down further within it until he can shepherd the new ribs of steel on to the end of the bridge. He bolts them in, having to free-fall in order to use all of his weight for the final turns of the giant wrench. He allows ten feet of loose rope on the pulley, attaches the wrench, then drops on to the two-foot handle, going down with it, and jars with the stiffening of the bolt, falling off into the air, and jars again when he reaches the end of the rope. He pulleys himself up and does it again. After ten minutes every bone feels broken—the air he stops in feels hard as concrete, his spine aching where the harness pulls him short.

He rises with the traveller from the lower level, calling out numbers to the driver above him through the fog, alongside the clattering of the woodwork he holds on to, the creaks and bends of the lattice drowning out his call of *one—two—three—four* which is the only language he uses. He was doing this once when a traveller collapsed at night— the whole structure—the rope shredding around him. He let go, swinging into the darkness, *anywhere* that might be free of the fifteen tons of falling timber which crashed onto the lower level and then tumbled down into the val- ley, rattling and banging in space like a trolley full of metal. And on the far end of the swing, he knew he had escaped the timber, but not necessarily the arm-thick wires that were now uncoiling free, snaking powerfully in every direction through the air. On his return swing he curled into a ball to avoid them, hearing the wires whip laterally as they completed the energy of the break. His predecessor had been killed in a similar accident, cut, the upper half of his body found an hour later, still hanging in the halter.

By eight a.m. the fog is burned up and the men have already been working for over two hours. A smell of tar descends to Nicholas as workers somewhere pour and begin to iron it level. He hangs waiting for the whistle that announces the next journey of the traveller. Below him is the Don River, the Grand Trunk, the CN and CP railway tracks, and Rosedale Valley Road. He can see the houses and work shacks, the beautiful wooden sheeting of the abutment which looks like a revival tent. Wind dries the sweat on him. He talks in English to himself.

*

She takes the first step out of the Ohrida Lake Restaurant into the blue corridor—the narrow blue lane of light that leads to the street. What she will become she becomes in that minute before she is outside, before she steps into the six-a.m. morning. The parrot Alicia regards her departure and then turns its attention back to the man asleep in the chair, one arm on the table, palm facing up as if awaiting donations, his head against the wall beside a crest. He is in darkness now, the open palm callused and hard. Five years earlier or ten years into the future the woman would have smelled the flour in his hair, his body having slept next to the dough, curling around it so his heat would make it rise. But now it was the hardness of his hands, the sound of them she would remember like wood against glass.

*

Commissioner Harris never speaks to Nicholas Temelcoff but watches often as he hooks up and walks at the viaduct edge listening to the engineer Taylor's various instructions. He appears abstracted but Harris knows he listens carefully. Nicholas never catches anyone's eye, as if he must hear the orders nakedly without seeing a face around the words.

His eyes hook to objects. Wood, a railing, a rope clip. He eats his sandwiches without looking at them, watching instead a man attaching a pulley to the elevated railings or studying the expensive leather on the shoes of the architects. He drinks water from a corked green bottle and his eyes are focused a hundred feet away. He never realizes how often he is watched by others. He has no clue that his gestures are extreme. He has no portrait of himself. So he appears to Harris and the others as a boy: say, a fanatic about toy cars, some stage they all passed through years ago.

Nicholas strides the parapet looking sideways at the loops of rope and then, without pausing, steps into the clear air. Now there is for Harris nothing to see but the fizzing rope, a quick slither. Nicholas stops twenty feet down with a thud against his heart. Sometimes on the work deck they will hear him slowly begin to sing various songs, breaking down syllables and walking around them as if laying the clauses out like tackle on a pavement to be checked for worthiness, picking up one he fancies for a moment then replacing it with another. As with sight, because Nicholas does not listen to most conversations around him, he assumes no one hears him.

For Nicholas language is much more difficult than what

he does in space. He loves his new language, the terrible barriers of it. *"'Does she love me?—Absolutely! Do I love her?—Positively!'"* Nicholas sings out to the forty-foot pipe he ferries across the air towards the traveller. *He* knows Harris. He *knows* Harris by the time it takes him to walk the sixty-four feet six inches from sidewalk to sidewalk on the bridge and by his expensive tweed coat that cost more than the combined weeks' salaries of five bridge workers.

The event that will light the way for immigration in North America is the talking picture. The silent film brings nothing but entertainment—a pie in the face, a fop being dragged by a bear out of a department store—all events governed by fate and timing, not language and argument. The tramp never changes the opinion of the policeman. The truncheon swings, the tramp scuttles through a corner window and disturbs the fat lady's ablutions. These comedies are nightmares. The audience emits horrified laughter as Chaplin, blindfolded, rollerskates near the edge of the unbalconied mezzanine. No one shouts to warn him. He cannot talk or listen. North America is still without language, gestures and work and bloodlines are the only currency.

But it was a spell of language that brought Nicholas here, arriving in Canada without a passport in 1914, a great journey made in silence. Hanging under the bridge, he describes the adventure to himself, just as he was told a fairy tale of Upper America by those who returned to the

Macedonian villages, those first travellers who were the
judas goats to the west.

Daniel Stoyanoff had tempted them all. In North America everything was rich and dangerous. You went in as a
sojourner and came back wealthy—Daniel buying a farm
with the compensation he had received for losing an arm
during an accident in a meat factory. Laughing about it!
Banging his other hand down hard onto the table and
wheezing with laughter, calling them all fools, sheep! As if
his arm had been a dry cow he had fooled the Canadians
with.

Nicholas had been stunned by the simplicity of the contract. He could see Stoyanoff's body livid on the killing
floor—standing in two inches of cow blood, screaming
like nothing as much as cattle, his arm gone, his balance
gone. He had returned to the village of Oschima, his
sleeve flapping like a scarf, and with cash for the land. He
had looked for a wife with two arms and settled down.

In ten years Daniel Stoyanoff had bored everyone in the
village with his tall tales and he couldn't wait for children to
grow up and become articulate so he could thrill them with
his sojourner's story of Upper America. What Daniel told
them was that he had in fact lost both arms in the accident,
but he happened to be rooming with a tailor who was out
of work and who had been, luckily, on the killing floors of
Schnaufer's that morning. Dedora the tailor had pulled gut
out of a passing cat, stitched Daniel's right arm back on,
and then turned for the other but a scrap dog had run off
with it, one of those dogs that lounged by the doorway.
Whenever you looked up from cutting and slicing the car-

casses you would see them, whenever you left work at the end of the day in your blood-soaked overalls and boots they followed you, licking and chewing your cuffs.

Stoyanoff's story was told to all children of the region at a certain age and he became a hero to them. *Look*, he would say, stripping off his shirt in the Oschima high street, irritating the customers of Petroff's outdoor bar once more, *look at what a good tailor Dedora was—no hint of stitches.* He drew an imaginary line around his good shoulder and the kids brought their eyes up close, then went over to his other shoulder and saw the alternative, the grotesque stump.

Nicholas was twenty-five years old when war in the Balkans began. After his village was burned he left with three friends on horseback. They rode one day and a whole night and another day down to Trikala, carrying food and a sack of clothes. Then they jumped on a train that was bound for Athens. Nicholas had a fever, he was delirious, needing air in the thick smoky compartments, wanting to climb up onto the roof. In Greece they bribed the captain of a boat a napoleon each to carry them over to Trieste. By now they all had fevers. They slept in the basement of a deserted factory, doing nothing, just trying to keep warm. There had to be no hint of illness before trying to get into Switzerland. They were six or seven days in the factory basement, unaware of time. One almost died from the high fevers. They slept embracing each other to keep warm. They talked about Daniel Stoyanoff's America.

On the train the Swiss doctor examined everyone's eyes

and let the four friends continue over the border. They were in France. In Le Havre they spoke to the captain of an old boat that carried animals. It was travelling to New Brunswick.

Two of Nicholas' friends died on the trip. An Italian showed him how to drink blood in the animal pens to keep strong. It was a French boat called *La Siciliana*. He still remembered the name, remembered landing in Saint John and everyone thinking how primitive it looked. How primitive Canada was. They had to walk half a mile to the station where they were to be examined. They took whatever they needed from the sacks of the two who had died and walked towards Canada.

Their boat had been so filthy they were covered with lice. The steerage passengers put down their baggage by the outdoor taps near the toilets. They stripped naked and stood in front of their partners as if looking into a mirror. They began to remove the lice from each other and washed the dirt off with cold water and a cloth, working down the body. It was late November. They put on their clothes and went into the Customs sheds.

Nicholas had no passport, he could not speak a word of English. He had ten napoleons, which he showed them to explain he wouldn't be dependent. They let him through. He was in Upper America.

He took a train for Toronto, where there were many from his village; he would not be among strangers. But there was no work. So he took a train north to Copper Cliff, near Sudbury, and worked there in a Macedonian bakery. He was paid seven dollars a month with food and sleeping quarters. After six months he went to Sault Ste. Marie. He still could hardly speak English and decided to go to school, working nights in another Macedonian bakery. If he did not learn the language he would be lost.

The school was free. The children in the class were ten years old and he was twenty-six. He used to get up at two in the morning and make dough and bake till 8:30. At nine he would go to school. The teachers were all young ladies and were very good people. During this time in the Sault he had translation dreams—because of his fast and obsessive studying of English. In the dreams trees changed not just their names but their looks and character. Men started answering in falsettos. Dogs spoke out fast to him as they passed him on the street.

When he returned to Toronto all he needed was a voice for all this language. Most immigrants learned their English from recorded songs or, until the talkies came, through mimicking actors on stage. It was a common habit to select one actor and follow him throughout his career, annoyed when he was given a small part, and seeing each of his plays as often as possible—sometimes as often as ten times during a run. Usually by the end of an east-end production at the Fox or Parrot Theatres the actors' speeches would be followed by growing echoes as Macedonians, Finns, and Greeks repeated the phrases after a half-second pause, trying to get the pronunciation right.

This infuriated the actors, especially when a line such as "Who put the stove in the living room, Kristin?"—which had originally brought the house down—was now spoken simultaneously by at least seventy people and so tended to lose its spontaneity. When the matinee idol Wayne Burnett dropped dead during a performance, a Sicilian butcher took over, knowing his lines and his blocking meticulously, and money did not have to be refunded.

Certain actors were popular because they spoke slowly. Lethargic ballads, and a kind of blues where the first line of a verse is repeated three times, were in great demand. Sojourners walked out of their accent into regional American voices. Nicholas, unfortunately, would later choose Fats Waller as his model and so his emphasis on usually unnoticed syllables and the throwaway lines made him seem high-strung or dangerously antisocial or too loving.

But during the time he worked on the bridge, he was seen as a recluse. He would begin sentences in his new language, mutter, and walk away. He became a vault of secrets and memories. Privacy was the only weight he carried. None of his cohorts really knew him. This man, awkward in groups, would walk off and leave strange clues about himself, like a dog's footprints on the snowed roof of a garage.

*

Hagh! A doctor attending his arm, this is what woke him, brought him out of his dream. *Hah!* It was six hours since he had fallen asleep. Kosta was there. He saw that the veil and his shirt had been cut open by the doctor. Somehow, they said, he had managed to get his arm back into the socket.

He jerked his hand to the veil, looking at it closely.

She had stayed until Kosta came down in the early

morning. She talked to him about the arm, to get a doctor, she had to leave. She spoke? Yes yes. What did she sound like? Hah? What more did Kosta know about her? He mentioned her black skirt. Before he left, Nicholas looked around the bar and found strips of the black habit she had cut away to make a skirt for the street.

When he walks into the fresh air outside the Ohrida Lake Restaurant, on the morning after the accident on the bridge, he sees the landscape as something altered, no longer so familiar that it is invisible to him. Nicholas Temelcoff walks now seeing Parliament Street from the point of view of the woman—who had looked through his belt-satchel while he slept, found his wide wire shears, and used them to cut away the black lengths of her habit. When he walks out of the Ohrida Lake Restaurant that morning it is her weather he grows aware of. He knows he will find her.

There are long courtships which are performed in absence. This one is built perhaps on his remark about her hair or her almost-silent question as he was falling off some tower or bridge into sleep. The verge of sleep was always terrifying to Nicholas so he would drink himself into it blunting out the seconds of pure fear when he could not use his arms, would lie there knowing he'd witness the half-second fall before sleep, the fear of it greater than anything he felt on the viaduct or any task he carried out for the Dominion Bridge Company.

As he fell, he remembers later, he felt a woman's arm reaching for him, curious about his name.

He is aware of her now, the twin. What holds them

together is not the act which saved her life but those moments since. The lost song on the radio. His offhand and relaxed flattery to a nun with regard to her beauty. Then he had leaned his head back, closed his eyes for too long, and slept.

A week later he rejoins the flatbed truck that carries the tar and fire, jumps on with the other men, and is back working at the bridge. His arm healed, he swings from Pier D to Pier C, ignores the stories he hears of the nun who disappeared. He lies supine on the end of his tether looking up towards the struts of the bridge, pivoting slowly. He knows the panorama of the valley better than any engineer. Like a bird. Better than Edmund Burke, the bridge's architect, or Harris, better than the surveyors of 1912 when they worked blind through the bush. The panorama revolves with him and he hangs in this long silent courtship, her absence making him look everywhere.

In a year he will open up a bakery with the money he has saved. He releases the catch on the pulley and slides free of the bridge.

ELIMINATION DANCE
(an intermission)

A crowded dance floor. The band halts in the middle of a number. The Master of Ceremonies steps to the microphone: "Any person who has had a tentative offer from Reader's Digest *to have their novel condensed." All dancers thus described retire. The music resumes, pauses again: "Women who have given up the accordian because of pinched breasts." In this way the ranks of the eliminated swell.*

"Elimination Dance" is based on those dances where a caller decides, seemingly randomly, who is forbidden to continue dancing. The last remaining couple wins a prize.

Those who are allergic to the sea

Those who have resisted depravity

Men who shave off beards in stages, pausing to take photographs

American rock stars who wear Toronto Maple Leaf hockey sweaters

Those who (while visiting a foreign country) have lost the end of a Q-Tip in their ear and have been unable to explain their problem

Gentlemen who have placed a microphone beside a naked woman's stomach after lunch and later, after slowing down the sound considerably, have sold these noises on the open market as whale songs

All actors and poets who spit into the first row while they perform

Anyone who has mistaken a flasher's penis for a loaf of bread while cycling through France

Men who fear to use an electric lawn-mower feeling they could drowse off and be dragged by it into a swimming pool

Any dinner guest who has consumed the host's missing contact lens with the dessert

Any person who has the following dream. You are in a subway station of a major city. At the far end you see a coffee machine. You put in two coins. The Holy Grail drops down. Then blood pours into the chalice

Any person who has lost a urine sample in the mail

Those who have noticed and then become obsessed with the fly crawling over Joan Fontaine's blouse during a key emotional scene in *September Affair*

Anyone who has had to step into an elevator with all of the Irish Rovers

Those who have filled in a bilingual and confidential pig survey from Statistics Canada. (Une enquête sur les porcs, strictement confidentielle)

Those who have written to the age old brotherhood of Rosicrucians for a free copy of their book *The Mastery of Life* in order to release the inner consciousness and to experience (in the privacy of the home) momentary flights of the soul

Those who have accidently stapled themselves

Anyone who has been penetrated by a mountie

Those currently working on a semaphore edition of *War and Peace*

Any university professor who has danced with a life-sized cardboard cut-out of Jean Genet

Those who have unintentionally locked themselves within a sleeping bag at a camping goods store

Those who, after a swim, find the sensation of water dribbling out of their ears erotic

Men who have never touched a whippet

Women who gave up the accordion because of pinched breasts

Those who have pissed out of the back of moving trucks

Those who have woken to find the wet footprints of a peacock across their kitchen floor

Anyone whose knees have been ruined as a result of performing sexual acts in elevators

Those who have so much as contemplated the possibility of creeping up to one's enemy with two Bic lighters, pressing simultaneously the butane switches—one into each nostril—and so gassing him to death

Literary critics who have swum the Hellespont

Any lover who has gone into a flower shop on Valentine's Day and asked for clitoris when he meant clematis

Anyone who has consumed a dog's heart pills during seasons of passion

Those who have come across their own telephone numbers underneath terse insults or compliments in the washroom of the Bay Street Bus Terminal

Those who have used the following techniques of seduction:
      –small talk at a falconry convention
      –entering a spa town disguised as Ford Madox Ford
      –making erotic rotations of the pelvis, backstage, during the storm scene of *King Lear*
      –underlining suggestive phrases in the prefaces of Joseph Conrad

Anyone who has testified as a character witness for a dog in a court of law

Any writer who has been photographed for the jacket of a book in one of the following poses: sitting in the back of a 1956 Dodge with two roosters; in a tuxedo with the Sydney Opera House in the distance; studying the vanishing point on a jar of Dutch Cleanser; against a gravestone with dramatic back lighting; with a false nose on; in the vicinity of Macchu Pichu; or sitting in a study and looking intensely at one's own book

The person who borrowed my Martin Beck thriller, read it in a sauna which melted the glue off the spine so the pages drifted to the floor, stapled them together and returned the book, thinking I wouldn't notice

Any person who has burst into tears at the Liquor Control Board

Anyone with pain

Katharine

from THE ENGLISH PATIENT

The first time she dreamed of him she woke up beside her husband screaming.

In their bedroom she stared down onto the sheet, mouth open. Her husband put his hand on her back.

"Nightmare. Don't worry."

"Yes."

"Shall I get you some water?"

"Yes."

She wouldn't move. Wouldn't lie back into that zone they had been in.

The dream had taken place in this room—his hand on her neck (she touched it now), his anger towards her that she had sensed the first few times she had met him. No, not anger, a lack of interest, irritation at a married woman being among them. They had been bent over like animals, and he had yoked her neck back so she had been unable to breathe within her arousal.

Her husband brought her the glass on a saucer but she could not lift her arms, they were shaking, loose. He put the glass awkwardly against her mouth so she could gulp the chlorinated water, some coming down her chin, falling to her stomach. When she lay back she hardly had time to think of what she had witnessed, she fell into a quick deep sleep.

That had been the first recognition. She remembered it sometime during the next day, but she was busy then and she refused to nestle with its significance for long, dismissed it; it was an accidental collision on a crowded night, nothing more.

A year later the other, more dangerous, peaceful dreams came. And even within the first one of these she recalled the hands at her neck and waited for the mood of calmness between them to swerve to violence.

Who lays the crumbs of food that tempt you? Towards a person you never considered. A dream. Then later another series of dreams.

He said later it was propinquity. Propinquity in the desert. It does that here, he said. He loved the word—the propinquity of water, the propinquity of two or three bodies in a car driving the Sand Sea for six hours. Her sweating knee beside the gearbox of the truck, the knee swerving, rising with the bumps. In the desert you have time to look everywhere, to theorize on the choreography of all things around you.

When he talked like that she hated him, her eyes remaining polite, her mind wanting to slap him. She always had the desire to slap him, and she realized even that was sexual. For him all relationships fell into patterns. You fell into propinquity or distance. Just as, for him, the histories in Herodotus clarified all societies. He assumed he was experienced in the ways of the world he had essentially left years earlier, struggling ever since to explore a half-invented world of the desert.

At Cairo aerodrome they loaded the equipment into the vehicles, her husband staying on to check the petrol lines of the Moth before the three men left the next morning. Madox went off to one of the embassies to send a wire. And *he* was going into town to get drunk, the usual final evening in Cairo, first at Madame Badin's Opera Casino, and later to disappear into the streets behind the Pasha Hotel. He would pack before the evening began, which would allow him to just climb into the truck the next morning, hung over.

So he drove her into town, the air humid, the traffic bad and slow because of the hour.

"It's so hot. I need a beer. Do you want one?"

"No, I have to arrange for a lot of things in the next couple of hours. You'll have to excuse me."

"That's all right," she said. "I don't want to interfere."

"I'll have one with you when I come back."

"In three weeks, right?"

"About that."

"I wish I were going too."

He said nothing in answer to that. They crossed the Bulaq Bridge and the traffic got worse. Too many carts, too many pedestrians who owned the streets. He cut south along the Nile towards the Semiramis Hotel, where she was staying, just beyond the barracks.

"You're going to find Zerzura this time, aren't you."

"I'm going to find it this time."

He was like his old self. He hardly looked at her on the drive, even when they were stalled for more than five minutes in one spot.

At the hotel he was excessively polite. When he behaved this way she liked him even less; they all had to pretend this pose was courtesy, graciousness. It reminded her of a dog in clothes. To hell with him. If her husband didn't have to work with him she would prefer not to see him again.

He pulled her pack out of the rear and was about to carry it into the lobby.

"Here, I can take that." Her shirt was damp at the back when she got out of the passenger seat.

The doorman offered to take the pack, but he said, "No, she wants to carry it," and she was angry again at his assumption. The doorman left them. She turned to him and he passed her the bag so she was facing him, both hands awkwardly carrying the heavy case in front of her.

"So. Good-bye. Good luck."

"Yes. I'll look after them all. They'll be safe."

She nodded. She was in shadow, and he, as if unaware of the harsh sunlight, stood in it.

Then he came up to her, closer, and she thought for a moment he was going to embrace her. Instead he put his right arm forward and drew it in a gesture across her bare neck so her skin was touched by the whole length of his damp forearm.

"Good-bye."

He walked back to the truck. She could feel his sweat

now, like blood left by a blade which the gesture of his arm seemed to have imitated.

She picks up a cushion and places it onto her lap as a shield against him. "If you make love to me I won't lie about it. If I make love to you I won't lie about it."

She moves the cushion against her heart, as if she would suffocate that part of herself which has broken free.

"What do you hate most?" he asks.

"A lie. And you?"

"Ownership," he says. "When you leave me, forget me."

Her fist swings towards him and hits hard into the bone just below his eye. She dresses and leaves.

Each day he would return home and look at the black bruise in the mirror. He became curious, not so much about the bruise, but about the shape of his face. The long eyebrows he had never really noticed before, the beginning of grey in his sandy hair. He had not looked at himself like this in a mirror for years. That was a long eyebrow.

Nothing can keep him from her.

When he is not in the desert with Madox or with Bermann in the Arab libraries, he meets her in Groppi Park—beside the heavily watered plum gardens. She is happiest here. She is a woman who misses moisture, who has always loved low green hedges and ferns. While for him this much greenery feels like a carnival.

From Groppi Park they arc out into the old city, South Cairo, markets where few Europeans go. In his rooms maps cover the walls. And in spite of his attempts at furnishing there is still a sense of base camp to his quarters.

They lie in each other's arms, the pulse and shadow of the fan on them. All morning he and Bermann have worked in the archaeological museum placing Arabic texts and European histories beside each other in an attempt to recognize echo, coincidence, name changes—back past Herodotus to the *Kitab al Kanuz*, where Zerzura is named after the bathing woman in a desert caravan. And there too the slow blink of a fan's shadow. And here too the intimate exchange and echo of childhood history, of scar, of manner of kiss.

"I don't know what to do. I don't know what to do! How can I be your lover? He will go mad."

A list of wounds.

The various colours of the bruise—bright russet leading to brown. The plate she walked across the room with, flinging its contents aside, and broke across his head, the blood rising up into the straw hair. The fork that entered the back of his shoulder, leaving its bite marks the doctor suspected were caused by a fox.

He would step into an embrace with her, glancing first to see what moveable objects were around. He would meet her with others in public with bruises or a bandaged head and explain about the taxi jerking to a halt so that he had hit the open side window. Or with iodine on his forearm that covered a welt. Madox worried about his becoming suddenly accident-prone. She sneered quietly at the weakness of his explanation. Maybe it's his age, maybe he needs glasses, said her husband, nudging Madox. Maybe it's a woman he met, she said. Look, isn't that a woman's scratch or bite?

It was a scorpion, he said. *Androctonus australis.*

A postcard. Neat handwriting fills the rectangle.

> *Half my days I cannot bear not to touch you.*
> *The rest of the time I feel it doesn't matter*
> *if I ever see you again. It isn't the morality,*
> *it is how much you can bear.*

No date, no name attached.

Sometimes when she is able to spend the night with him they are wakened by the three minarets of the city beginning their prayers before dawn. He walks with her through the indigo markets that lie between South Cairo and her home. The beautiful songs of faith enter the air like arrows, one minaret answering another, as if passing on a rumour of the two of them as they walk through the cold morning air, the smell of charcoal and hemp already making the air profound. Sinners in a holy city.

He sweeps his arm across plates and glasses on a restaurant table so she might look up somewhere else in the city hearing this cause of noise. When he is without her. He, who has never felt alone in the miles of longitude between desert towns. A man in a desert can hold absence in his cupped hands knowing it is something that feeds him more than water. There is a plant he knows of near El Taj, whose heart, if one cuts it out, is replaced with a fluid containing herbal goodness. Every morning one can drink the liquid the amount of a missing heart. The plant continues to flourish for a year before it dies from some lack or other.

He lies in his room surrounded by the pale maps. He is without Katharine. His hunger wishes to burn down all social rules, all courtesy.

Her life with others no longer interests him. He wants only her stalking beauty, her theatre of expressions. He wants the minute and secret reflection between them, the depth of field minimal, their foreignness intimate like two pages of a closed book.

He has been disassembled by her.

And if she has brought him to this, what has he brought her to?

When she is within the wall of her class and he is beside her in larger groups he tells jokes he doesn't laugh at himself. Uncharacteristically manic, he attacks the history of exploration. When he is unhappy he does this. Only Madox recognizes the habit. But she will not even catch his eye. She smiles to everyone, to the objects in the room, praises a flower arrangement, worthless impersonal things. She misinterprets his behaviour, assuming this is what he wants, and doubles the size of the wall to protect herself.

But now he cannot bear this wall in her. You built your walls too, she tells him, so I have my wall. She says it glittering in a beauty he cannot stand. She with her beautiful clothes, with her pale face that laughs at everyone who smiles at her, with the uncertain grin for his angry jokes. He continues his appalling statements about this and that in some expedition they are all familiar with.

The minute she turns away from him in the lobby of Groppi's bar after he greets her, he is insane. He knows the only way he can accept losing her is if he can continue to hold her or be held by her. If they can somehow nurse each other out of this. Not with a wall.

Sunlight pours into his Cairo room. His hand flabby over the Herodotus journal, all the tension in the rest of his body, so he writes words down wrong, the pen sprawling as if without spine. He can hardly write down the word *sunlight*. The words *in love*.

In the apartment there is light only from the river and the desert beyond it. It falls upon her neck her feet the vaccination scar he loves on her right arm. She sits on the bed hugging nakedness. He slides his open palm along the sweat of her shoulder. This is my shoulder, he thinks, not her husband's, this is my shoulder. As lovers they have offered parts of their bodies to each other, like this. In this room on the periphery of the river.

In the few hours they have, the room has darkened to this pitch of light. Just river and desert light. Only when there is the rare shock of rain do they go towards the window and put their arms out, stretching, to bathe as much as they can of themselves in it. Shouts towards the brief down-pour fill the streets.

"We will never love each other again. We can never see each other again."

"I know," he says.

The night of her insistence on parting.

She sits, enclosed within herself, in the armour of her terrible conscience. He is unable to reach through it. Only his body is close to her.

"Never again. Whatever happens."

"Yes."

"I think he will go mad. Do you understand?"

He says nothing, abandoning the attempt to pull her within him.

An hour later they walk into a dry night. They can hear the gramophone songs in the distance from the Music for All cinema, its windows open for the heat. They will have to part before that closes up and people she might know emerge from there.

They are in the botanical garden, near the Cathedral of All Saints. She sees one tear and leans forward and licks it, taking it into her mouth. As she has taken the blood from his hand when he cut himself cooking for her. Blood. Tear. He feels everything is missing from his body, feels he contains smoke. All that is alive is the knowledge of future desire and want. What he would say he cannot say to this woman whose openness is like a wound, whose youth is not mortal yet. He cannot alter what he loves most in her, her lack of compromise, where the romance of the poems she loves still sits with ease in the real world. Outside these qualities he knows there is no order in the world.

This night of her insistence. Twenty-eighth of September. The rain in the trees already dried by hot moonlight. Not one cool drop to fall down upon him like a tear. This parting at Groppi Park. He has not asked if her husband is home in that high square of light, across the street.

He sees the tall row of traveller's palms above them, their outstretched wrists. The way her head and hair were above him, when she was his lover.

Now there is no kiss. Just one embrace. He untugs himself from her and walks away, then turns. She is still there. He comes back within a few yards of her, one finger raised to make a point.

"I just want you to know. I don't miss you yet."

His face awful to her, trying to smile. Her head sweeps away from him and hits the side of the gatepost. He sees it hurt her, notices the wince. But they have separated already into themselves now, the walls up at her insistence. Her jerk, her pain, is accidental, is intentional. Her hand is near her temple.

"You will," she says.

From this point on in our lives, she had whispered to him earlier, we will either find or lose our souls.

How does this happen? To fall in love and be disassembled.

I was in her arms. I had pushed the sleeve of her shirt up

to the shoulder so I could see her vaccination scar. I love this, I said. This pale aureole on her arm. I see the instrument scratch and then punch the serum within her and then release itself, free of her skin, years ago, when she was nine years old, in a school gymnasium.

In Situ

Westbury, England, 1940

Kirpal Singh stood where the horse's saddle would have lain across its back. At first he simply stood on the back of the horse, paused and waved to those he could not see but who he knew would be watching. Lord Suffolk watched him through binoculars, saw the young man wave, both arms up and swaying.

Then he descended, down into the giant white chalk horse of Westbury, into the whiteness of the horse, carved into the hill. Now he was a black figure, the background radicalizing the darkness of his skin and his khaki uniform. If the focus on the binoculars was exact, Lord Suffolk would see the thin line of crimson lanyard on Singh's shoulder that signalled his sapper unit. To them it would look like he was striding down a paper map cut out in the shape of an animal. But Singh was conscious only of his boots scuffing the rough white chalk as he moved down the slope.

Miss Morden, behind him, was also coming slowly down

the hill, a satchel over her shoulder, aiding herself with a rolled umbrella. She stopped ten feet above the horse, unfurled the umbrella and sat within its shade. Then she opened up her notebooks.

"Can you hear me?" he asked.

"Yes, it's fine." She rubbed the chalk off her hands onto her skirt and adjusted her glasses. She looked up into the distance and, as Singh had done, waved to those she could not see.

Singh liked her. She was in effect the first Englishwoman he had really spoken with since he arrived in England. Most of his time had been spent in a barracks at Woolwich. In his three months there he had met only other Indians and English officers. A woman would reply to a question in the NAAFI canteen, but conversations with women lasted only two or three sentences.

He was the second son. The oldest son would go into the army, the next brother would be a doctor, a brother after that would become a businessman. An old tradition in his family. But all that had changed with the war. He joined a Sikh regiment and was shipped to England. After the first months in London he had volunteered himself into a unit of engineers that had been set up to deal with delayed-action and unexploded bombs. The word from on high in 1939 was naive: *"Unexploded bombs are considered the responsibility of the Home Office, who are agreed that they should be collected by A.R.P. wardens and police and delivered to convenient dumps, where members of the armed forces will in due course detonate them."*

It was not until 1940 that the War Office took over

responsibility for bomb disposal, and then, in turn, handed it over to the Royal Engineers. Twenty-five bomb disposal units were set up. They lacked technical equipment and had in their possession only hammers, chisels and road-mending tools. There were no specialists.

Eighty percent of bombs dropped by airplanes over Britain were thin-walled, general-purpose bombs. They usually ranged from a hundred pounds to a thousand. A 2,000-pound bomb was called a "Hermann" or an "Esau." A 4,000-pound bomb was called a "Satan."

Singh, after long days of training, would fall asleep with diagrams and charts still in his hands. Half dreaming, he entered the maze of a cylinder alongside the picric acid and the gaine and the condensers until he reached the fuze deep within the main body. Then he was suddenly awake.

When a bomb hit a target, the resistance caused a trembler to activate and ignite the flash pellet in the fuze. The minute explosion would leap into the gaine, causing the penthrite wax to detonate. This set off the picric acid, which in turn caused the main filling of TNT, amatol and aluminized powder, to explode. The journey from trembler to explosion lasted a microsecond.

The most dangerous bombs were those dropped from low altitudes, which were not activated until they had landed. These unexploded bombs buried themselves in cities and fields and remained dormant until their trembler contacts were disturbed—by a farmer's stick, a car wheel's nudge, the bounce of a tennis ball against the casing—and then they would explode.

Singh was moved by lorry with the other volunteers to the research department in Woolwich. This was a time when the casualty rate in bomb disposal units was appallingly high, considering how few unexploded bombs there were. In 1940, after France had fallen and Britain was in a state of siege, it got worse.

By August the blitz had begun, and in one month there were suddenly 2,500 unexploded bombs to be dealt with. Roads were closed, factories deserted. By September the number of live bombs had reached 3,700. One hundred new bomb squads were set up, but there was still no understanding of how the bombs worked. Life expectancy in these units was ten weeks.

In the car, driving down to Westbury, Singh had sat in front with Mr. Harts while Miss Morden rode in the back with Lord Suffolk. The khaki-painted Humber was famous. The mudguards were painted bright signal red—as all bomb disposal travel units were—and at night there was a blue filter over the left sidelight. Two days earlier a man walking near the famous chalk horse on the Downs had been blown up. When engineers arrived at the site they discovered that another bomb had landed in the middle of the historic location—in the stomach of the giant white horse of Westbury carved into the rolling chalk hills in 1778. Shortly after this event, all the chalk horses on the Downs—there were seven—had camouflage nets pegged down over them, not to protect them so much as stop them being obvious landmarks for bombing raids over England.

From the backseat Lord Suffolk chatted about the migration of robins from the war zones of Europe, the history of bomb disposal, Devon cream. He was introducing the customs of England to the young Sikh as if it was a recently discovered culture. In spite of being Lord Suffolk he lived in Devon, and until war broke out his passion was the study of *Lorna Doone* and how authentic the novel was historically and geographically. Most winters he spent puttering around the villages of Brandon and Porlock, and he had convinced authorities that Exmoor was an ideal location for bomb-disposal training. There were twelve men under his command—made up of talents from various units, sappers and engineers, and Singh was one of them. They were based for most of the week at Richmond Park in London, being briefed on new methods or working on unexploded bombs while fallow deer drifted around them. But on weekends they would go down to Exmoor, where they would continue training during the day and afterwards be driven by Lord Suffolk to the church where Lorna Doone was shot during her wedding ceremony. "Either from this window or from that back door . . . shot right down the aisle—into her shoulder. Splendid shot, actually, though of course reprehensible. The villain was chased onto the moors and had his muscles ripped from his body." To Singh it sounded like a familiar Indian fable.

Lord Suffolk's closest friend in the area was a female aviator who hated society but loved Lord Suffolk. They went shooting together. She lived in a small cottage in Countisbury on a cliff that overlooked the Bristol Channel. Each village they passed in the Humber had its exotica described by Lord Suffolk. "This is the very best place to buy blackthorn walking sticks." As if Singh were thinking of stepping into the Tudor corner store in his uniform and turban to chat casually with the owners about canes. Lord Suffolk was the best of the English, he later told Hana. If there had been no war he would never have roused himself from Countisbury and his retreat, called Home Farm, where he mulled along with the wine, with the flies in the old back laundry, fifty years old, married but essentially bachelor in character, walking the cliffs each day to visit his aviator friend. He liked to fix things—old laundry tubs and plumbing generators and cooking spits run by a waterwheel. He had been helping Miss Swift, the aviator, collect information on the habits of badgers.

The drive to the chalk horse at Westbury was therefore busy with anecdote and information. Even in wartime he knew the best place to stop for tea. He swept into Pamela's Tea Room, his arm in a sling from an accident with guncotton, and shepherded in his clan—secretary, chauffeur and sapper—as if they were his children. How Lord Suffolk had persuaded the UXB Committee to allow him to set up his experimental bomb disposal outfit no one was sure, but with his background in inventions he probably had more qualifications than most. He was an autodidact, and he believed his mind could read the motives and spirit behind any invention. He had immediately invented the pocket shirt, which allowed fuzes and gadgets to be stored easily by a working sapper.

They drank tea and waited for scones, discussing the in situ defusing of bombs.

"I trust you, Mr. Singh, you know that, don't you?"

"Yes, sir." Singh adored him. As far as he was concerned, Lord Suffolk was the first real gentleman he had met in England.

"You know I trust you to do as well as I. Miss Morden will be with you to take notes. Mr. Harts will be farther back. If you need more equipment or more strength, blow on the police whistle and he will join you. He doesn't advise but he understands perfectly. If he won't do something it means he disagrees with you, and I'd take his advice. But you have total authority on the site. Here is my pistol. The fuzes are probably more sophisticated now, but you never know, you might be in luck."

Lord Suffolk was alluding to an incident that had made him famous. He had discovered a method for inhibiting a delayed-action fuze by pulling out his army revolver and firing a bullet through the fuze head, so arresting the movement of the clock body. The method was abandoned when the Germans introduced a new fuze in which the percussion cap and not the clock was uppermost.

Kirpal Singh had been befriended, and he would never forget it. So far, half of his time during the war had taken place in the slipstream of this lord who had never stepped out of England and planned never to step out of Countisbury once the war ended. Singh had arrived in England knowing no one, distanced from his family in the Punjab. He was twenty-one years old. He had met no one but soldiers. So that when he read the notice asking for volunteers with an experimental bomb squad, even though he heard other sappers speak of Lord Suffolk as a madman, he had already decided that in a war you have to take control, and there was a greater chance of choice and life alongside a personality or an individual.

He was the only Indian among the applicants, and Lord Suffolk was late. Fifteen of them were led into a library and asked by the secretary to wait. She remained at the desk, copying out names, while the soldiers joked about the interview and the test. He knew no one. He walked over to a wall and stared at a barometer, was about to touch it but pulled back, just putting his face close to it. *Very Dry* to *Fair* to *Stormy.* He muttered the words to himself with his new English pronunciation. "Wery dry. *Very* dry." He looked back at the others, peered around the room and caught the gaze of the middle-aged secretary. She watched him sternly. An Indian boy. He smiled and walked towards the bookshelves. Again he touched nothing. At one point he put his nose close to a volume called *Raymond, or Life and Death* by Sir Oliver Hodge. He found another, similar title. *Pierre, or the Ambiguities.* He turned and caught the woman's eyes on him again. He felt as guilty as if he had put the book in his pocket. She had probably never seen a turban before. The English! They expect you to fight for them but won't talk to you. Singh. And the ambiguities.

They met a very hearty Lord Suffolk during lunch, who poured wine for anyone who wanted it, and laughed loudly at every attempt at a joke by the recruits. In the afternoon they were all given a strange exam in which a piece of machinery had to be put back together without any prior information of what it was used for. They were allowed two hours but could leave as soon as the problem was solved. Singh finished the exam quickly and spent the rest of the time inventing other objects that could be made from the various components. He sensed he would be admitted easily if it were not for his race. He had come from a country where mathematics and mechanics were natural traits. Cars were never destroyed. Parts of them were carried across a village and readapted into a sewing machine or water pump. The backseat of a Ford was reupholstered and became a sofa. Most people in his village were more likely to carry a spanner or screwdriver than a pencil. A car's irrelevant parts thus entered a grandfather clock or irrigation pulley or the spinning mechanism of an office chair. Antidotes to mechanized disaster were easily found. One cooled an overheating car engine not with new rubber hoses but by scooping up cow shit and patting it around the condenser. What he saw in England was a surfeit of parts that would keep the continent of India going for two hundred years.

He was one of three applicants selected by Lord Suffolk. This man who had not even spoken to him (and had not laughed with him, simply because he had not joked) walked across the room and put his arm around his shoulder. The severe secretary turned out to be Miss Morden, and she bustled in with a tray that held two large glasses of sherry, handed one to Lord Suffolk and, saying, "I know you don't drink," took the other one for herself and raised her glass to him. "Congratulations, your exam was splendid. Though I was sure you would be chosen, even before you took it."

"Miss Morden is a splendid judge of character. She has a nose for brilliance and character."

"Character, sir?"

"Yes. It is not really necessary, of course, but we *are* going to be working together. We are very much a family here. Even before lunch Miss Morden had selected you."

"I found it quite a strain being unable to wink at you, Mr. Singh."

Lord Suffolk had his arm around Singh again and was walking him to the window.

"I thought, as we do not have to begin till the middle of next week, I'd have some of the unit come down to Home Farm. We can pool our knowledge in Devon and get to know each other. You can drive down with us in the Humber."

So he had won passage, free of the chaotic machinery of the war. He stepped into a family, after a year abroad, as if he were the prodigal returned, offered a chair at the table, embraced with conversations.

It was almost dark when they crossed the border from Somerset into Devon on the coastal road overlooking the Bristol Channel. Mr. Harts turned down the narrow path bordered with heather and rhododendrons, a dark blood colour in this last light. The driveway was three miles long.

Apart from the trinity of Suffolk, Morden and Harts,

there were six sappers who made up the unit. They walked the moors around the stone cottage over the weekend. Miss Morden and Lord Suffolk and his wife were joined by the aviatrix for the Saturday-night dinner. Miss Swift told Singh she had always wished to fly overland to India. Removed from his barracks, Singh had no idea of his location. There was a map on a roller high up on the ceiling. Alone one morning he pulled the roller down until it touched the floor. *Coutisbury and Area. Mapped by R. Fones. Drawn by desire of Mr. James Halliday.*

"Drawn by desire . . ." He was beginning to love the English.

He is with Hana in the night tent when he tells her about the explosion in Erith. A 250-kilogram bomb erupting as Lord Suffolk attempted to dismantle it. It also killed Mr. Fred Harts and Miss Morden and four sappers Lord Suffolk was training. May 1941. Singh had been with Suffolk's unit for a year. He was working in London that day with Lieutenant Blackler, clearing the Elephant and Castle area of a Satan bomb. They had worked together at defusing the 4,000-pound bomb and were exhausted. He remembered halfway through he looked up and saw a couple of bomb disposal officers pointing in his direction and wondered what that was about. It probably meant they had found another bomb. It was after ten at night and he was dangerously tired. There was another one waiting for him. He turned back to work.

When they had finished with the Satan he decided to

save time and walked over to one of the officers, who had at first half turned away as if wanting to leave.

"Yes. Where is it?"

The man took his right hand, and he knew something was wrong. Lieutenant Blackler was behind him and the officer told them what had happened, and Lieutenant Blackler put his hands on Singh's shoulders and gripped him.

He drove to Erith. He had guessed what the officer was hesitating about asking him. He knew the man would not have come there just to tell him of the deaths. They were in a war, after all. It meant there was a second bomb somewhere in the vicinity, probably the same design, and this was the only chance to find out what had gone wrong.

He wanted to do this alone. Lieutenant Blackler would stay in London. They were the last two left of the unit, and it would have been foolish to risk both. If Lord Suffolk had failed, it meant there was something new. He wanted to do this alone, in any case. When two men worked together there had to be a base of logic. You had to share and compromise decisions.

He kept everything back from the surface of his emotions during the night drive. To keep his mind clear, they still had to be alive. Miss Morden drinking one large and stiff whisky before she got to the sherry. In this way she would be able to drink more slowly, appear more ladylike for the rest of the evening. "You don't drink, Mr. Singh, but if you did, you'd do what I do. One full whisky and then you can sip away like a good courtier." This was followed by her lazy, gravelly laugh. She was the only woman he was to meet in his life who carried two silver flasks with her. So she was still drinking, and Lord Suffolk was still nibbling at his Kipling cakes.

The other bomb had fallen half a mile away. Another SC-250kg. It looked like the familiar kind. They had defused hundreds of them, most by rote. This was the way the war progressed. Every six months or so the enemy altered something. You learned the trick, the whim, the little descant, and taught it to the rest of the units. They were at a new stage now.

He took no one with him. He would just have to remember each step. The sergeant who drove him was a man named Hardy, and he was to remain by the jeep. It was suggested he wait till the next morning, but he knew they would prefer him to do it now. The 250-kilogram SC was too common. If there was an alteration they had to know quickly. He made them telephone ahead for lights. He didn't mind working tired, but he wanted proper lights, not just the beams of two jeeps.

When he arrived in Erith the bomb zone was already lit. In daylight, on an innocent day, it would have been a field. Hedges, perhaps a pond. Now it was an arena. Cold, he borrowed Hardy's sweater and put it on top of his. The lights would keep him warm, anyway. When he walked over to the bomb they were still alive in his mind. Exam.

With the bright light, the porousness of the metal jumped into precise focus. Now he forgot everything except distrust. Lord Suffolk had said you can have a brilliant chess player at seventeen, even thirteen, who might beat a grand master. But you can never have a brilliant bridge player at that age. Bridge depends on character. Your character and the character of your opponents. You must consider the character of your enemy. This is true of bomb disposal. It is two-handed bridge. You have one enemy. You have no partner. Sometimes for my exam I make them play bridge. People think a bomb is a mechanical object, a mechanical enemy. But you have to consider that somebody made it.

The wall of the bomb had been torn open in its fall to earth, and Singh could see the explosive material inside. He felt he was being watched, and refused to decide whether it was by Suffolk or the inventor of this contraption. The freshness of the artificial light had revived him. He walked around the bomb, peering at it from every angle. To re-move the fuze, he would have to open the main chamber and get past the explosive. He unbuttoned his satchel and, with a universal key, carefully twisted off the plate at the back of the bomb case. Looking inside he saw that the fuze pocket had been knocked free of the case. This was good luck—or bad luck; he couldn't tell yet. The problem was that he didn't know if the mechanism was already at work, if it had already been triggered. He was on his knees, lean-ing over it, glad he was alone, back in the world of straight-forward choice. Turn left or turn right. Cut this or cut that. But he was tired, and there was still anger in him.

He didn't know how long he had. There was more dan-ger in waiting too long. Holding the nose of the cylinder firm with his boots, he reached in and ripped out the fuze pocket, and lifted it away from the bomb. As soon as he did this he began to shake. He had got it out. The bomb was essentially harmless now. He put the fuze with its tangled fringe of wires down on the grass; they were clear and brilliant in this light.

He started to drag the main case towards the truck, fifty yards away, where the men could empty it of the raw explosive. As he pulled it along, a third bomb exploded a quarter of a mile away and the sky lit up, making even the arc lights seem subtle and human.

An officer gave him a mug of Horlicks, which had some kind of alcohol in it, and he returned alone to the fuze pocket. He inhaled the fumes from the drink.

There was no longer serious danger. If he were wrong, the small explosion would take off his hand. But unless it was clutched to his heart at the moment of impact he wouldn't die. The problem was now simply the problem. The fuze. The new "joke" in the bomb.

He would have to reestablish the maze of wires into its original pattern. He walked back to the officer and asked him for the rest of the Thermos of the hot drink. Then he returned and sat down again with the fuze. It was about one-thirty in the morning. He guessed, he wasn't wearing a watch. For half an hour he just looked at it with a magnified circle of glass, a sort of monocle that hung off his buttonhole. He bent over and peered at the brass for any hint of other scratches that a clamp might have made. Nothing.

Later he would need distractions. Later, when there was a whole personal history of events and moments in his mind, he would need something equivalent to white sound to burn or bury everything while he thought of the problems in front of him. The radio or crystal set and its loud band music would come later, a tarpaulin to hold the rain of real life away from him.

But now he was aware of something in the far distance, like some reflection of lightning on a cloud. Harts and Morden and Suffolk were dead, suddenly just names. His eyes focused back onto the fuze box.

He began to turn the fuze upside down in his mind, considering the logical possibilities. Then turned it horizontal again. He unscrewed the gaine, bending over, his ear next to it so the scrape of brass was against him. No little clicks. It came apart in silence. Tenderly he separated the clockwork sections from the fuze and set them down. He picked up the fuze-pocket tube and peered down into it again. He saw nothing. He was about to lay it on the grass when he hesitated and brought it back up to the light. He wouldn't have noticed anything wrong except for the weight. And he would never have thought about the weight if he wasn't looking for the joke. All they did, usually, was listen or look. He tilted the tube carefully, and the weight slipped down toward the opening. It was a second gaine—a whole separate device—to foil any attempt at defusing.

He eased the device out towards him and unscrewed the gaine. There was a white-green flash and the sound of a whip from the device. The second detonator had gone off. He pulled it out and set it beside the other parts on the grass. He went back to the jeep.

"There was a second gaine," he muttered. "I was very lucky, being able to pull out those wires. Put a call in to headquarters and find out if there are other bombs."

He cleared the soldiers away from the jeep, set up a loose

bench there and asked for the arc lights to be trained on it. He bent down and picked up the three components and placed them each a foot apart along the makeshift bench. He was cold now, and he breathed out a feather of his warmer body air. He looked up. In the distance some soldiers were still emptying out the main explosive. Quickly he wrote down a few notes and handed the solution for the new bomb to an officer. He didn't fully understand it, of course, but they would have this information.

When sunlight enters a room where there is a fire, the fire will go out. He had loved Lord Suffolk and his strange bits of information. But his absence here, in the sense that everything now depended on Singh, meant Singh's awareness swelled to all bombs of this variety across the city of London. He had suddenly a map of responsibility, something, he realized, that Lord Suffolk carried within his character at all times. It was this awareness that later created the need in him to block so much out when he was working on a bomb. He was one of those never interested in the choreography of power. He felt uncomfortable in the ferrying back and forth of plans and solutions. He felt capable only of reconnaissance, of locating a solution. When the reality of the death of Lord Suffolk came to him, he concluded the work he was assigned to and reenlisted into the anonymous machine of the army. He was on the troopship *Macdonald*, which carried a hundred other sappers towards the Italian campaign. Here they were used not just for bombs but for building bridges, clearing debris, setting up tracks for armoured rail vehicles. He hid there for the rest of the war. Few remembered the Sikh who had been with

Suffolk's unit. In a year the whole unit was disbanded and forgotten, Lieutenant Blackler being the only one to rise in the ranks with his talent.

But that night as Singh drove past Lewisham and Black-heath towards Erith, he knew he contained, more than any other sapper, the knowledge of Lord Suffolk. He was expected to be the replacing vision.

He was still standing at the truck when he heard the whistle that meant they were turning off the arc lights. Within thirty seconds metallic light had been replaced with sulphur flares in the back of the truck. Another bomb raid. These lesser lights could be doused when they heard the planes. He sat down on the empty petrol can facing the three components he had removed from the SC-250kg, the hisses from the flares around him loud after the silence of the arc lights.

He sat watching and listening, waiting for them to click. The other men silent, fifty yards away. He knew he was for now a king, a puppet master, could order anything, a bucket of sand, a fruit pie for his needs, and those men who would not cross an uncrowded bar to speak with him when they were off duty would do what he desired. It was strange to him. As if he had been handed a large suit of clothes that he could roll around in and whose sleeves would drag behind him. But he knew he did not like it. He was accustomed to his invisibility. In England he was ignored in the various barracks, and he came to prefer that. The self-sufficiency and privacy Hana saw in him later were caused not just by his being a sapper in the Italian campaign. It was as much a result of being the anonymous member of another race, a part of the invisible world. He had built up defences of character against all that, trusting only those who befriended him. But that night in Erith he knew he was capable of having wires attached to him that influenced all around him who did not have his specific talent.

A few months later he had escaped to Italy, had packed the shadow of his teacher into a knapsack, the way he had seen the green-clothed boy at the Hippodrome do it on his first leave during Christmas. Lord Suffolk and Miss Morden had offered to take him to an English play. He had selected *Peter Pan*, and they, wordless, acquiesced and went with him to a screaming child-full show. There were such shadows of memory with him when he lay in his tent with Hana in the small hill town in Italy.

Revealing his past or qualities of his character would have been too loud a gesture. Just as he could never turn and inquire of her what deepest motive caused this relationship. He held her with the same strength of love he felt for those three strange English people, eating at the same table with them, who had watched his delight and laughter and wonder when the green boy raised his arms and flew into the darkness high above the stage, returning to teach the young girl in the earthbound family such wonders too.

In the flare-lit darkness of Erith he would stop whenever planes were heard, and one by one the sulphur torches were sunk into buckets of sand. He would sit in the droning darkness, moving the seat so he could lean forward and place his ear close to the ticking mechanisms, still timing the clicks, trying to hear them under the throb of the German bombers above him.

Then what he had been waiting for happened. After exactly one hour, the timer tripped and the percussion cap exploded. Removing the main gaine had released an unseen striker that activated the second, hidden gaine. It had been set to explode sixty minutes later—long after a sapper would normally have assumed the bomb was safely defused.

This new device would change the whole direction of Allied bomb disposal. From now on, every delayed-action bomb would carry the threat of a second gaine. It would no longer be possible for sappers to deactivate a bomb by simply removing the fuze. Bombs would have to be neutralized with the fuze intact. Somehow, earlier on, surrounded by arc lights, and in his fury, he had withdrawn the sheared second fuze out of the booby trap. In the sulphureous darkness under the bombing raid he witnessed the white-green flash the size of his hand. One hour late. He had survived only with luck. He walked back to the officer and said, "I need another fuze to make sure."

They lit the flares around him again. Once more light poured into his circle of darkness. He kept testing the new fuzes for two more hours that night. The sixty-minute delay proved to be consistent.

He was in Erith most of that night. In the morning he woke up to find himself back in London. He could not remember being driven back. He woke up, went to a table and began to sketch the profile of the bomb, the gaines, the detonators, the whole ZUS-40 problem, from the fuze up to the locking rings. Then he covered the basic drawing with all the possible lines of attack to defuse it. Every arrow drawn exactly, the text written out clear the way he had been taught.

What he had discovered the night before held true. He had survived only through luck. There was no possible way to defuse such a bomb in situ without just blowing it up. He drew and wrote out everything he knew on the large blueprint sheet. At the bottom he wrote: *Drawn by desire of Lord Suffolk, by his student Lieutenant Kirpal Singh, 10 May 1941.*

He worked flat-out, crazily, after Suffolk's death. Bombs were altering fast, with new techniques and devices. He was barracked in Regent's Park with Lieutenant Blackler and three other specialists, working on solutions, blue-printing each new bomb as it came in.

In twelve days, working at the Directorate of Scientific Research, they came up with the answer. Ignore the fuze entirely. Ignore the first principle, which until then was "defuse the bomb." It was brilliant. They were all laughing and applauding and hugging each other in the officers' mess. They didn't have a clue what the alternative was, but they knew in the abstract they were right. The problem would not be solved by embracing it. That was Lieutenant Blackler's line. "If you are in a room with a problem don't talk to it." An offhand remark. Singh came towards him and held the statement from another angle. "Then we don't touch the fuze at all."

Once they came up with that, someone worked out the solution in a week. A steam sterilizer. One could cut a hole into the main case of a bomb, and then the main explosive could be emulsified by an injection of steam and drained away. That solved that for the time being. But by then he was on a ship to Italy.

He keeps remembering one thing. He is in the white horse. He feels hot on the chalk hill, the white dust of it swirling up all around him. He works on the contraption, which is quite straightforward, but for the first time he is working alone. Miss Morden sits twenty yards above him, higher up the slope, taking notes on what he is doing. He knows that down and across the valley Lord Suffolk is watching through the glasses.

He works slowly. The chalk dust lifts, then settles on everything, his hands, the contraption, so he has to blow it off the fuze caps and wires continually to see the details. It is hot in the tunic. He keeps putting his sweating wrists behind himself to wipe them on the back of his shirt. All the loose and removed parts fill the various pockets across his chest. He is tired, checking things repetitively. He hears Miss Morden's voice. "Kip?" "Yes." "Stop what you're doing for a while, I'm coming down." "You'd better not, Miss Morden." "Of course I can." He does up the buttons on his various vest pockets and lays a cloth over the bomb; she clambers down into the white horse awkwardly and then sits next to him and opens up her satchel. She douses a lace handkerchief with the contents of a small bottle of eau de cologne and passes it to him. "Wipe your face with this. Lord Suffolk uses it to refresh himself." He takes it tentatively and at her suggestion dabs his forehead and neck and wrists. She unscrews the Thermos and pours each of them some tea. She unwraps oil paper and brings out strips of Kipling cake.

She seems to be in no hurry to go back up the slope, back to safety. And it would seem rude to remind her that she should return. She simply talks about the wretched heat and the fact that at least they have booked rooms in town with baths attached, which they can all look forward to. She begins a rambling story about how she met Lord Suffolk. Not a word about the bomb beside them. He had been slowing down, the way one, half asleep, continually rereads the same paragraph, trying to find a connection between sentences. She had pulled him out of the vortex of the problem. She packs up her satchel carefully, lays a hand on his right shoulder and returns to her position on the blanket above the Westbury horse. She leaves him some sunglasses, but he cannot see clearly enough through them so he lays them aside. Then he goes back to work. The scent of eau de cologne. He remembers he had smelled it once as a child. He had a fever and someone had brushed it onto his body.

THE GREAT TREE

"Zou Fulei died like a dragon breaking down a wall . . .

this line composed and ribboned
in cursive script
by his friend the poet Yang Weizhen

whose father built a library
surrounded by hundreds of plum trees

It was Zou Fulei, almost unknown,
who made the best plum flower painting
of any period

One branch lifted into the wind

and his friend's vertical line of character

their tones of ink
—wet to opaque
dark to pale

each sweep and gesture
trained and various
echoing the other's art

In the high plum-surrounded library
where Yang Weizhen studied as a boy

a moveable staircase was pulled away
to ensure his solitary concentration

His great work
"untrammelled" "eccentric" "unorthodox"
"no taint of the superficial"
     "no flamboyant movement"

using at times the lifted tails
of archaic script,

sharing with Zou Fulei
his leaps and darknesses

*

"So I have always held you in my heart . . .

The great 14th-century poet calligrapher
mourns the death of his friend

Language attacks the paper from the air

There is only a path of blossoms

no flamboyant movement

A night of smoky ink in 1361
a night without a staircase

TO A SAD DAUGHTER

All night long the hockey pictures
gaze down at you
sleeping in your tracksuit.
Belligerent goalies are your ideal.
Threats of being traded
cuts and wounds
—all this pleases you.
O my god! you say at breakfast
reading the sports page over the Alpen
as another player breaks his ankle
or assaults the coach.

When I thought of daughters
I wasn't expecting this
but I like this more.
I like all your faults
even your purple moods
when you retreat from everyone
to sit in bed under a quilt.
And when I say "like"

I mean of course "love"
but that embarrasses you.
You who feel superior to black and white movies
(coaxed for hours to see *Casablanca*)
though you were moved
by *Creature from the Black Lagoon.*

One day I'll come swimming
beside your ship or someone will
and if you hear the siren
listen to it. For if you close your ears
only nothing happens. You will never change.

I don't care if you risk
your life to angry goalies
creatures with webbed feet.
You can enter their caves and castles
their glass laboratories. Just
don't be fooled by anyone but yourself.

This is the first lecture I've given you.
You're "sweet sixteen" you said.
I'd rather be your closest friend
than your father. I'm not good at advice
you know that, but ride
the ceremonies
until they grow dark.

Sometimes you are so busy
discovering your friends

I ache with a loss
—but that is greed.
And sometimes I've gone
into *my* purple world
and lost you.

One afternoon I stepped
into your room. You were sitting
at the desk where I now write this.
Forsythia outside the window
and sun spilled over you
like a thick yellow miracle
as if another planet
was coaxing you out of the house
—all those possible worlds!—
and you, meanwhile, busy with mathematics.

I cannot look at forsythia now
without loss, or joy for you.
You step delicately
into the wild world
and your real prize will be
the frantic search.
Want everything. If you break
break going out not in.
How you live your life I don't care
but I'll sell my arms for you,
hold your secrets for ever.

If I speak of death
which you fear now, greatly,
it is without answers,
except that each
one we know is
in our blood.
Don't recall graves.
Memory is permanent.
Remember the afternoon's
yellow suburban annunciation.
Your goalie
in his frightening mask
dreams perhaps
of gentleness.

THE STORY

for Akash and Kamlesh Mishra

i

For his first forty days a child
is given dreams of previous lives.
Journeys, winding paths,
a hundred small lessons
and then the past is erased.

Some are born screaming,
some full of introspective wandering
into the past—that bus ride in winter,
the sudden arrival within
a new city in the dark.
And those departures from family bonds
leaving what was lost and needed.
So the child's face is a lake
of fast moving clouds and emotions.

A last chance for the clear history of the self.
All our mothers and grandparents here,

our dismantled childhoods
in the buildings of the past.

Some great forty-day daydream
before we bury the maps.

ii

There will be a war, the king told his pregnant wife.
In the last phase seven of us will cross
the river to the east and disguise ourselves
through the farmlands.
We will approach the markets
and befriend the rope-makers. Remember this.

She nods and strokes the baby in her belly.

After a month we will enter
the halls of that king.
There is dim light from small high windows.
We have entered with no weapons,
just rope in the baskets.
We have trained for years
to move in silence, invisible,
not one creak of bone,
not one breath,
even in lit rooms,
in order to disappear into this building
where the guards live in half-light.

When a certain night falls
the seven must enter the horizontal door
remember this, face down,
as in birth.

Then (he tells his wife)
there is the corridor of dripping water,
a noisy rain, a sense
of creatures at your feet.
And we enter halls of further darkness,
cold and wet among the enemy warriors.
To overcome them we douse the last light.

After battle we must leave another way
avoiding all doors to the north . . .

(The king looks down
and sees his wife is asleep
in the middle of the adventure.

He bends down and kisses through the skin
the child in the body of his wife.
Both of them in dreams. He lies there,
watches her face as it catches a breath.
He pulls back a wisp across her eye
and bites it off. Braids it
into his own hair, then sleeps beside them.)

iii

With all the swerves of history
I cannot imagine your future.
Would wish to dream it, see you
in your teens, as I saw my son,
your already philosophical air
rubbing against the speed of the city.
I no longer guess a future.
And do not know how we end
nor where.

Though I know a story about maps, for you.

iv

After the death of his father,
the prince leads his warriors
into another country.
Four men and three women.
They disguise themselves and travel
through farms, fields of turnip.
They are private and shy
in an unknown, uncaught way.

In the hemp markets
they court friends.
They are dancers who tumble
with lightness as they move,

their long hair wild in the air.
Their shyness slips away.

They are charming with desire in them.
It is the dancing they are known for.

One night they leave their beds.
Four men, three women.
They cross open fields where nothing grows
and swim across the cold rivers
into the city.

Silent, invisible among the guards,
they enter the horizontal door
face down so the blades of poison
do not touch them. Then
into the rain of the tunnels.

It is an old story—that one of them
remembers the path in.
They enter the last room of faint light
and douse the lamp. They move
within the darkness like dancers
at the centre of a maze
seeing the enemy before them
with the unlit habit of their journey.

There is no way to behave after victory.

And what should occur now is unremembered.

The seven stand there.
One among them, who was that baby,
cannot recall the rest of the story
—the story his father knew, unfinished
that night, his mother sleeping.

We remember it as a tender story,
though perhaps they perish.
The father's lean arm across
the child's shape, the taste
of the wisp of hair in his mouth . . .

The seven embrace in the destroyed room
where they will die without
the dream of exit.
We do not know what happened.
From the high windows the ropes
are not long enough to reach the ground.
They take up the knives of the enemy
and cut their long hair and braid it
onto one rope and they descend
hoping it will be long enough
into the darkness of the night.

STEP

The ceremonial funeral structure for a monk
made up of thambili palms, white cloth
is only a vessel, disintegrates

completely as his life.

The ending disappears,
replacing itself

with something abstract
as air, a view.

All we'll remember in the last hours
is an afternoon—a lazy lunch
then sleeping together.

Then the disarray of grief.

On the morning of a full moon
in a forest monastery
thirty women in white
meditate on the precepts of the day
until darkness.

They walk those abstract paths
their complete heart
their burning thought focused
on this step, then *this* step.

In the red brick dusk
of the Sacred Quadrangle,
among holy seven-storey ambitions
where the four Buddhas
of Polonnaruwa
face out to each horizon,
is a lotus pavilion.

Taller than a man
nine lotus stalks of stone
stand solitary in the grass,
pillars that once supported
the floor of another level.

(The sensuous stalk
the sacred flower)

How physical yearning
became permanent.

How desire became devotional
so it held up your house,
your lover's house, the house of your god.

And though it is no longer there,
the pillars once let you step
to a higher room
where there was worship, lighter air.

Linus Corea

from ANIL'S GHOST

A few years earlier a story had gone around about a Colombo doctor—Linus Corea—a neurosurgeon in the private sector. He came from three generations of doctors, the family name was as established as the most permanent banks in Sri Lanka. Linus Corea was in his late forties when the war broke out. Like most doctors he thought it was madness and unlike most he stayed in private practice; the Prime Minister was one of his clients, as was the leader of the opposition. He had his head massages at Gabriel's at eight a.m. and saw his patients from nine till two, then golfed with a bodyguard at his side. He dined out, got home before curfew and slept in an air-conditioned room. He had been married for ten years and had two sons. He was a well-liked man; he was polite with everyone because it was the easiest way not to have trouble, to be invisible to those who did not matter to him. This small courtesy created a bubble he rode within. His gestures and politeness disguised an essential lack of interest or, if not that, a lack of time for others on the street. He liked photography. He printed his own pictures in the evening.

In 1987, while he was putting on a golf green, his bodyguard was shot dead and Dr. Linus Corea was kidnapped. They came out of the woods slowly, unconcerned about being seen by him. It meant it did not matter to them and that frightened him more than anything. He had been alone with the bodyguard. He stood beside the prone body and was surrounded by the men who had shot him from a distance of forty yards precisely through the correct point in the head. No thrashing around.

They spoke to him calmly in a made-up language, which again increased his anxiety. They hit him once and broke a rib to warn him to behave, and then they walked back to their car and drove away with him. For months no one knew where he had got to. The police, the Prime Minister, the head of the Communist Party were called in, and all were outraged. There was no communication from kidnappers wanting payment. It was the Colombo mystery of 1987, and offers of rewards were made throughout the press, none of which was answered.

Eight months after Linus Corea's disappearance, his wife was alone in the house with their two children when a man came to the door and handed her a letter from her husband. The man stepped inside. The note was simple. It said: *If you wish to see me again, come with the children. If you do not wish to, I will understand.*

She moved to the phone, and the man produced a gun. She stood there. To her left was a pool where some flowers floated in shallow water. All her valuables were upstairs. She stood there, the children busy in their rooms. It had not been a joyous marriage. Comfortable but not happy.

Affections on the thin scale of things. But the letter, while it held his terseness, had a quality she would never have expected. It gave her a choice. It was laconically stated but it was there, graciously, with no strings. Later she thought that if it had not been for that she would not have gone. She muttered to the man. He spoke back to her in an invented language that she did not understand. Some of the news reports at the time of her husband's disappearance had spoken of UFO kidnappings, and this strangely came to her mind now, there in her front hall.

"We'll come with you," she said again, out loud, and this time the man came towards her and gave her another letter.

This one was just as abrupt and said: *Please bring these books.* A list followed, eight titles. He told her where they could be found in his office. She told her sons to get a few extra clothes and shoes, but she packed nothing for herself. She carried only the books, and once they were outside the man directed them to an already humming car.

Linus Corea made his way to the tent in the dark and lay down on the cot. It was nine at night, and if they came they would be there in about five hours. He had told the men when it was most likely for her to be home alone. He needed to sleep. He had been working in the triage tent for close to six hours, so even with the brief nap after lunch he was exhausted.

He had been at the camp of the insurgents ever since they had picked him up in Colombo. They had got him a little after two in the afternoon and by seven he was in the southern hills. No one had spoken to him in the car, just the idiot language, a joke of theirs. What good it did he wasn't sure. When he reached the camp they explained in Sinhala what they wanted him to do, which was to work as a doctor for them. Nothing more. It was not an intense conversation, he wasn't threatened. They told him he could see his family in a few months. They said he could sleep now but in the morning he would have to work. A few hours later they woke him and said there was an emergency, and led him into the triage tent with a lantern and hung it on a hook above a half-dead body and asked him to operate on the skull in lamplight. The man was too far gone, still they asked him to operate. He himself was uncomfortable with his broken rib and whenever he leaned forward pain tore through him. Half an hour later the man died and they carried the lantern to another bed, where someone else who had been shot had been waiting in silence. He had to remove the leg above the knee, but the man lived. Linus Corea went back to sleep at two-thirty. At six a.m. they woke him again to begin work.

After a few days he asked them to get some smocks for him, some rubber gloves, some morphine. He gave them a list of things he needed, and that night they attacked a hospital near Gurutulawa and got the medical essentials and kidnapped a nurse for him. She too, strangely, did not complain about her fate, just as he hadn't. Privately he was irritated, and tired of a world that necessitated this, but the device of courtesy that had been false in his other life continued. He thanked people for nothing much and he didn't ask for anything unless it was badly needed. He became accustomed to this lack of need, was rather proud of it. If he wanted something—syringes, bandages, a book—he would write out a list and give it to them. Maybe a week later, maybe six weeks, he'd get them. The first hospital attack was the only one they planned just for him.

He did not know how long they would keep him so he began to teach the nurse everything he could about surgery. Rosalyn was about forty, very smart under her seeming complacency. He had her operating alongside him when they were overrun with wounded.

After the first month he admitted to himself that he didn't miss his children or wife anymore, even that much of Colombo. Not that he was happy here, but being busy he was preoccupied.

There was no energy in him to be angry or insulted. Six till noon. Two hours off for lunch and sleep. Then he worked six more hours. If there was a crisis he worked longer. The nurse was always beside him. She wore one of the smocks that he had requested and was very proud of it, washing it out every evening so it would be clean in the morning.

He was asleep when his family arrived. The nurse tried to wake him, but he was dead to the world. She suggested that the wife come into her tent with the two boys so he could sleep undisturbed, he had to be up in a few hours to work. At what? the wife said. He's a doctor, the nurse said.

It was just as well. The drive had been arduous and she and the children were tired themselves. This was not the time to greet and talk. When they woke the next morning it was ten, and her husband had already been working for four hours. Had walked into their tent carrying his mug of tea, looked at them, and then had gone to work with the nurse. The nurse had told him she was surprised his wife was that young, and the doctor had laughed. In Colombo he would have reddened or become angry. He was aware this nurse could say anything to him.

So when his wife and children woke they were ignored. The nurse was gone, the soldiers they saw went their own way. The mother insisted they stay together, and they went searching around the compound like lost tourists till they found the nurse washing bandages outside a dirty tent.

Rosalyn came up to him and said something he did not catch and she repeated it, that his wife and children were by the tent entrance. He looked up, then asked her if she could take over, and she nodded. He walked away from the close focus of the tent work, passed people lying on the ground, towards his wife and the children. The nurse could see him almost bouncing with pleasure. When he came closer his wife saw the blood on his smock and she hesitated. "It doesn't matter," he said, lifting her into an embrace. She touched his beard, which he had forgotten he had grown. There were no mirrors and he hadn't seen it.

"You met Rosalyn?"

"Yes. She helped us last night. You of course wouldn't wake up."

"Mmm." Linus Corea laughed. "They keep me going." He paused, then said, "It's my life."

Anil

Anil had come out of her first class at Guy's Hospital in London with just one sentence in her exercise book: *The bone of choice would be the femur.*

She loved the way the lecturer had stated it, offhand, but with the air of a pompatus. As if this piece of information were the first rule needed before they could progress to greater principles. Forensic studies began with that one thighbone.

What surprised Anil as the teacher delineated the curriculum and the field of study was the quietness of the English classroom. In Colombo there was always a racket. Birds, lorries, fighting dogs, a kindergarten's lessons of rote, street salesmen—all their sounds entered through open windows. There was no chance of an ivory tower existing in the tropics. Anil wrote Dr. Endicott's sentence down and a few minutes later underlined it with her ballpoint in the hushed quiet. For the rest of the hour she just listened and watched the lecturer's mannerisms.

It was while studying at Guy's that Anil found herself in the smoke of one bad marriage. She was in her early twenties and was to hide this episode from everyone she met later in life. Even now she wouldn't replay it and consider the level of damage. She saw it more as some contemporary fable of warning.

He too was from Sri Lanka, and in retrospect she could see that she had begun loving him because of her loneliness. She could cook a curry with him. She could refer to a specific barber in Bambalapitiya, could whisper her desire for jaggery or jakfruit and be understood. That made a difference in the new, too brittle country. Perhaps she herself was too tense with uncertainty and shyness. She had expected to feel alien in England only for a few weeks. Uncles who had made the same journey a generation earlier had spoken romantically of their time abroad. They suggested that the right remark or gesture would open all doors. Her father's friend Dr. P. R. C. Peterson had told the story of being sent to school in England as an eleven-year-old. On the first day he was called a "native" by a classmate. He stood up at once and announced to the teacher, "I'm sorry to say this, sir, but Roxborough doesn't know who I am. He called me a 'native.' That's the wrong thing to do. *He* is the native and I'm the visitor to the country."

But acceptance was harder than that. Having been a mild celebrity in Colombo because of her swimming, Anil was shy without the presence of her talent, and found it difficult to enter conversations. Later, when she developed her gift for forensic work, she knew one of the advantages was that her skill signalled her existence—like a neutral herald.

In her first month in London she'd been constantly confused by the geography around her. (What she kept noticing about Guy's Hospital was the number of doors!) She missed two classes in her first week, unable to find the lecture room. So for a while she began arriving early each morning and waited on the front steps for Dr. Endicott, following him through the swing doors, stairways, grey-and-pink corridors, to the unmarked classroom. (She once followed him and startled him and others in the men's bathroom.)

She seemed timid even to herself. She felt lost and emotional. She murmured to herself the way one of her spinster aunts did. She didn't eat much for a week and saved enough money to phone Colombo. Her father was out and her mother was unable to come to the phone. It was about one in the morning and she had woken her *ayah*, Lalitha. They talked for a few minutes, until they were both weeping, it felt, at the far ends of the world. A month later she fell within the spell of her future, and soon-to-be, and eventually ex-, husband.

It seemed to her he had turned up from Sri Lanka in bangles and on stilts. He too was a medical student. He was not shy. Within days of their meeting he focussed his wits entirely on Anil—a many-armed seducer and note writer and flower bringer and telephone-message leaver (he had quickly charmed her landlady). His organized passion surrounded her. She had the sense that he had never been lonely or alone before meeting her. He had panache in the way he could entice and choreograph the other medical students. He was funny. He had cigarettes. She saw how he mythologized their rugby positions and included such things in the fabric of their conversations until they were familiar touchstones—a trick that never left any of them at a loss for words. A team, a gang, that was in fact only two weeks deep. They each had an epithet. Lawrence who had thrown up once on the Underground, the siblings Sandra and Percy Lewis whose family scandals were acknowledged and forgiven, Jackman of the wide brows.

He and Anil were married quickly. She briefly suspected that for him it was another excuse for a party that would bond them all. He was a fervent lover, even with his public life to choreograph. He certainly opened up the geography of the bedroom, insisting on lovemaking in their non-soundproof living room, on the wobbly sink in the shared bathroom down the hall, on the boundary line quite near the long-stop during a county cricket match. These private acts in an almost public sphere echoed his social nature. There seemed to be no difference for him between privacy and friendship with acquaintances. Later she would read that this was the central quality of a monster. Still, there was considerable pleasure on both their parts during this early period. Though she realized it was going to be crucial for her to come back to earth, to continue her academic studies.

When her father-in-law visited England he swept them up and took them out to dinner. The son was for once quiet, and the father attempted to persuade them to return to Colombo and have his grandchildren. He kept referring to himself as a philanthropist, which appeared to give him a belief that he was always on higher moral ground. As the dinner progressed she felt that every trick in the Colombo Seven social book was being used against her. He objected to her having a full-time career, keeping her own name, was annoyed at her talking back. When she described class-

room autopsies during the trifle, the father had been outraged. "Is there nothing you won't do?" And she had
replied, "I won't go to crap games with barons and earls."

The next day the father lunched alone with his son,
then flew back to Colombo.

At home the two of them fought now over everything.
She was suspicious of his insights and understanding. He
appeared to spend all his spare energy on empathy. When
she wept, he would weep. She never trusted weepers after
that. (Later, in the American Southwest, she would avoid
those television shows with weeping cowboys and weeping
priests.) During this time of claustrophobia and marital
warfare, sex was the only mutual constant. She insisted on
it as much as he. She assumed it gave the relationship some
normality. Days of battle and fuck.

The disintegration of the relationship was so certain on
her part that she would never replay any of their days
together. She had been fooled by energy and charm; he
had wept and burrowed under her intelligence until she
felt she had none left. Venus, as Sarath would say, had been
in her head, when it should have been the time of Jupiter.

She would return from the lab in the evenings and be
met by his jealousy. At first this presented itself as sexual
jealousy, then she saw it was an attempt to limit her
research and studies. It was the first handcuff of marriage,
and it almost buried her in their small flat in Ladbroke
Grove. After she escaped him she would never say his name
out loud. If she saw his handwriting on a letter she never
opened it, fear and claustrophobia rising within her. In
fact, the only reference to the era of her marriage she

allowed into her life was Van Morrison's "Slim Slow Slider" with its mention of Ladbroke Grove. Only the song survived. And only because it referred to separation.

> *Saw you early this morning*
> *With your brand-new boy and your Cadillac . . .*

She would sing along hoping that he did not also join in with his sentimental heart, wherever he was.

> *You've gone for something,*
> *And I know you won't be back.*

Otherwise the whole marriage and divorce, the hello and good-bye, she treated as something illicit that deeply embarrassed her. She left him as soon as their term at Guy's Hospital was over, so he could not locate her. She had plotted her departure for the end of term to avoid the harassment he was fully capable of; he was one of those men with time on his hands. *Cease and desist!* she had scrawled formally on his last little whining billet-doux before mailing it back to him.

She emerged with no partner. Cloudless at last. She was unable to bear the free months before she could begin classes again, before she could draw her studies close to her, more intimately and seriously than she had imagined possible. When she did return she fell in love with working at night, and sometimes she couldn't bear to leave the lab, just rested her happily tired dark head on the table. There was no curfew or compromise with a lover anymore. She got home at midnight, was up at eight, every casebook and experiment and investigation alive in her head and reachable.

Eventually she heard he'd returned to Colombo. And with his departure there was no longer any need to remember favourite barbers and restaurants along the Galle Road. Her last conversation in Sinhala was the distressed chat she'd had with Lalitha that ended with her crying about missing egg *rulang* and curd with jaggery. She no longer spoke Sinhala to anyone. She turned fully to the place she found herself in, focussing on anatomical pathology and other branches of forensics, practically memorizing Spitz and Fisher. Later she won a scholarship to study in the United States, and in Oklahoma became caught up in the application of the forensic sciences to human rights. Two years later, in Arizona, she was studying the physical and chemical changes that occurred in bones not only during life but also after death and burial.

She was now alongside the language of science. The femur was the bone of choice.

*

It was in the Arizona labs that Anil met and worked with a woman named Leaf. A few years older, Leaf became Anil's closest friend and constant companion. They worked side by side and they talked continually on the phone to each other when one was on assignment elsewhere. Leaf Niedecker—what kind of name is *that*, Anil had demanded to know—introduced Anil to the finer arts of ten-pin bowling, raucous hooting in bars, and high-speed driving in the desert, swerving back and forth in the night. *"Tenga cuidado con los armadillos, señorita."*

Leaf loved movies and remained in depression about the disappearance of drive-ins and their al fresco quality. "All our shoes off, all our shirts off, rolling against Chevy leather—there has been nothing like it since." So two or three times a week Anil would buy a barbequed chicken and arrive at Leaf's rented house. The television had already been carried into the yard and sat baldly beside a yucca tree. They'd rent *The Searchers* or any other John Ford or Fred Zinnemann movie. They watched *The Nun's Story*, *From Here to Eternity*, *Five Days One Summer*, sitting in Leaf's lawn chairs, or curled up beside each other in the double hammock, watching the calm, carefully sexual black-and-white walk of Montgomery Clift.

Nights in Leaf's backyard, once upon a time in the West. The heat still in the air at midnight. They would pause the movie, take a break and cool off under the garden hose. In three months they managed to see the complete oeuvres of Angie Dickinson and Warren Oates. "I'm asthmatic," Leaf said. "I need to become a cowboy."

They shared a joint and disappeared into the intricacies of *Red River*, theorizing on the strangely casual shooting of John Ireland before the final fight between Montgomery Clift and John Wayne. They rewound the video and watched it once more. Wayne swirling around gracefully, hardly interrupting his walk, to shoot a neutral friend who was trying to stop a fight. On their knees in the parched grass by the television screen they looked at the scene frame by frame for any sign of outrage at this unfairness on the victim's face. There seemed to be none. It was a minor act directed towards a minor character that may or may not have ended the man's life, and no one said anything about it during the remaining five minutes of the film. One of those Jacobean happy endings.

"I don't think the bullet killed him."

"Well, we can't tell where it hit him, Hawks goes off too quickly. The guy just puts his hand up to his stomach and then drops."

"If he got hit in the liver he's had it. Don't forget, this is Missouri in eighteen-fuck-knows-when."

"Yeah. What's his name?"

"Who?"

"The guy shot."

"Valance. Cherry Valance."

"Cherry? You mean like Jerry, or Cherry, like apple."

"Cherry Valance, not Apple Valance."

"And he's Montgomery's friend."

"Yeah, Montgomery's friend Cherry."

"Hmm."

"I don't think it hit him in the liver. Look at the angle of the shot. The trajectory seems to be going up. Popped a rib, I suspect, or glanced off it."

". . . Maybe glanced off and killed some woman on the sidewalk?"

"Or Walter Brennan . . ."

"No, some dame on the sidewalk that Howard Hawks was fucking."

"Women remember. Don't they know that? Those saloon girls are gonna remember Cherry. . . ."

"You know, Leaf, we should do a book. *A Forensic Doctor Looks at the Movies.*"

"The film noir ones are tough. Their clothes are baggy, it's too dark."

"I'm doing *Spartacus.*"

In Sri Lankan movie theatres, Anil told Leaf, if there was a great scene—usually a musical number or an extravagant fight—the crowd would yell out "Replay! Replay!" or "Rewind! Rewind!" till the theatre manager and projectionist were forced to comply. Now, on a smaller scale, the films staggered backwards and forwards, in Leaf's yard, until the actions became clear to them.

The film they worried over most was *Point Blank.* At the start of the movie, Lee Marvin (who once played Liberty Valance, no relation) is shot by a double-crossing friend in the abandoned Alcatraz prison. The friend leaves him for dead and steals his girl and his share of the money. Vengeance results. Anil and Leaf composed a letter to the director of the film, asking if he remembered, all these years later, where on the torso he imagined Lee Marvin was shot so that he could get to his feet, stagger through the prison while the opening credits came up and swim the treacherous waters between the island and San Francisco.

They told the director that it was one of their *favourite* films, they were simply inquiring as forensic specialists. When they looked at the scene closely they saw Lee Marvin's hand leap up to his chest. "See, he has difficulty on his right side. When he swims later in the bay he uses his left arm." "God, it's a great movie."

LAST INK

In certain countries aromas pierce the heart and one dies
half waking in the night as an owl and a murderer's cart go by

the way someone in your life will talk out love and grief
then leave your company laughing.

In certain languages the calligraphy celebrates
where you met the plum blossom and moon by chance

—the dusk light, the cloud pattern,
recorded always in your heart

and the rest of the world—chaos,
circling your winter boat.

Night of the Plum and Moon.

Years later you shared it
on a scroll or nudged

the ink onto stone
to hold the vista of a life.

A condensary of time in the mountains
—your rain-swollen gate, a summer
scarce with human meeting.
Just bells from another village.

The memory of a woman walking down stairs.

*

Life on an ancient leaf
or a crowded 5th-century seal

 this mirror-world of art
—lying on it as if a bed.

 When you first saw her,
the night of moon and plum,
you could speak of this to no one.
You cut your desire
against a river stone.
You caught yourself
in a cicada-wing rubbing,
lightly inked.
The indelible darker self.

 A seal, the Masters said,
must contain bowing and leaping,
"and that which hides in waters."

 Yellow, drunk with ink,
the scroll unrolls to the west

a river journey, each story
an owl in the dark, its child-howl

unreachable now
—that father and daughter,
that lover walking naked down blue stairs
each step jarring the humming from her mouth.

I want to die on your chest but not yet,
she wrote, sometime in the 13th century
of our love

before the yellow age of paper

before her story became a song,
lost in imprecise reproductions

until caught in jade,

whose spectrum could hold the black greens
the chalk-blue of her eyes in daylight.

＊

Our altering love, our moonless faith.

Last ink in the pen.

My body on this hard bed.

The moment in the heart
where I roam restless, searching

for the thin border of the fence
to break through or leap.

Leaping and bowing.

Anil's Ghost

This powerful novel transports us to Sri Lanka, a country steeped in centuries of tradition, now forced into the modern world by the ravages of civil war. Into this maelstrom steps Anil Tissera, a young woman born in Sri Lanka, educated in England and America, who returns to her homeland as a forensic anthropologist sent by an international human rights group to discover the source of the organized campaigns of murder engulfing the island. *Anil's Ghost* is a literary spellbinder.

Fiction/Literature/0-375-72437-0

The Cinnamon Peeler

An electrifying volume of stylish yet endlessly surprising poetry exploring friendship and passion, family history and personal mythology. Spanning twenty-seven years, *The Cinnamon Peeler* is a masterpiece of intelligence and ardor, informed by rueful wit, sensitivity to nature, and an exultant love of language.

Poetry/0-679-77913-2

The Collected Works of Billy the Kid

The Collected Works of Billy the Kid is a visionary novel about an icon of American violence. Drawing on contemporary accounts, period photographs, dime novels, and his own prodigious fund of empathy and imagination, Michael Ondaatje traces Billy's passage across the blasted landscape of 1880 New Mexico and the collective unconscious of his country.

Fiction/Literature/0-679-76786-X

Coming Through Slaughter

This novel brings to life the fabulous, colorful panorama of New Orleans in the first flush of the jazz era. It is the story of Buddy Bolden, the first of the great trumpet players, some say the originator of jazz, who was a genius, a guiding spirit, and the king of that time and place.

Fiction/Literature/0-679-76785-1

The English Patient

During the final moments of World War II, four damaged people come together in a deserted Italian villa. As their stories unfold, a complex tapestry of image and emotion is woven, leaving them inextricably connected by the brutal circumstances of the war. Winner of the Booker Prize.

Fiction/Literature/0-679-74520-3

Handwriting

Handwriting is a collection of exquisitely crafted poems of delicacy and power—poems about love, landscape, and the sweep of history set in the poet's first home, Sri Lanka. The falling away of culture is juxtaposed with an individual's sense of loss, grief, and remembrance as Ondaatje weaves a rich tapestry of images.

Poetry/0-375-70541-4

In the Skin of a Lion

This is the story of Patrick Lewis, a backwoods Canadian immigrant who arrives in 1920s Toronto and earns a living searching for a vanished millionaire and tunneling beneath Lake Ontario. In the course of his adventures, Patrick's life intersects with those of characters who reappear in *The English Patient.*

Fiction/Literature/0-679-77266-9

Running in the Family

In the late 1970s, Michael Ondaatje returned to his native country of Sri Lanka. Recording his journey through the drug-like heat and intoxicating fragrances of the island, Ondaatje simultaneously retraces the baroque mythology of his Dutch–Ceylonese family.

Memoir/Literature/0-679-74669-2

VINTAGE **READERS**

Authors available in this series

Martin Amis

Nicholson Baker

James Baldwin

A. S. Byatt

Willa Cather

Sandra Cisneros

Joan Didion

Richard Ford

Langston Hughes

Barry Lopez

Alice Munro

Haruki Murakami

Vladimir Nabokov

V. S. Naipaul

Michael Ondaatje

Oliver Sacks

*Representing a wide spectrum of some of our most significant
modern authors, the Vintage Readers offer an attractive,
accessible selection of writing that matters.*